GIRL
IN THE
WALL

Copyright © 2022 by Marilyn Gottlieb

All rights reserved, including the right to reproduce this book or portions thereof in any form whatsoever.

Published by:
The Crescendo Group
Quogue, New York

This is a work of fiction. Names, characters, places and incidents either are the product of the author's imagination or are used fictitiously.

Available from www.amazon.com and other retailers.

ISBN: 978-0-9890061-6-3

Girl in the Wall

This book is dedicated to my cousin, Suzanne Klein,
for sharing memories of summers at her parents' hotel,
the St. Regis, in Fleischmanns, NY

Marilyn   Suzy

and to
my husband, Frank J. Levy,
for reading numerous versions
of every chapter.

1. Down Comes the Wall

Momism: Expect the unexpected.

My perfect nose job and I had a simple plan. I would manage an upscale boutique where women of a certain age—my age—could find clothes that fit in the chest and hips. I hoped this new venture would fill the vacancy that left me searching for more meaning in the middle of my life while I struggled to fight aging. A skeleton was not part of the plan.

My husband, Kevin, a well-known plastic surgeon, funded what he called my "little project." A bit condescending, though much appreciated. He was busy filling faces with Botox and Juvederm, tucking in tummies and slicing years off people in the operating room. Our marketing maven and newly married daughter, Jennifer, and our son, Sean, in medical school, had little need for mothering.

My family couldn't help erase the useless feelings I had since my high-powered, corporate job had been taken from me. At first, I visited museums, met friends for lunch, did charity work and shopped. Then my days were spent home alone with our Golden Retriever, Max. I sulked for months, walking in circles around our apartment, yearning for the daily routine of my beloved career.

I know I sounded like a spoiled brat, in good health with no financial worries. Despite having a cushy life, at age 55, I wanted to feel valued with a new professional identity.

"Professional identity? That's ridiculous," Kevin had said with his arms around me. "You've already succeeded in business. You're my wife, my beautiful babe. You've raised two kids. Isn't that enough identity?"

"No," I said, pulling away. "How can you be so clueless?"

Susan, if you're going to do something, do it grand, Mom said in my head. Though she passed away years ago, my mother still has a way of inserting herself.

Following her advice, I rented two adjoining stores in a not so new townhouse nestled between high rise buildings on Madison Avenue less than a mile south of our apartment on Park and 80th. There were two floors above the store, each with one apartment. I didn't know who lived there, nor did I care. My interest revolved around the neighboring places that carried luxury brands like Dolce & Gabbana, Valentino and my favorite, Max Mara. I expected their customers to wander into my shop.

My designer, Francesca, had flown in from Italy. Though we barely knew each other, I invited her to stay with us, especially since her husband, Roberto, remained at home. He was a Rossano Brazzi look-alike, a man way too flirtatious who made me think of the 1954 film, *Three Coins in the Fountain*. I thought it best not to face him again considering our awkward history in Florence six months ago.

Today, my biggest challenge was to form one seamless store out of the two. Since my construction crew was scheduled to tear down the connecting wall, Francesca and I decided to check on their progress.

"What are ya crazy, ladies?" one worker said. "You can't come in now. It's hazardous."

"I'm paying for this job. You have to let me in," I said, wishing I had brought some cookies as a friendly gesture.

"Nobody cares if you're payin' for the whole damn building. You get hurt, we get sued. You're not comin' in here on my watch."

Even the foreman wouldn't allow us in—something about fines and stringent city regulations. He didn't know I rarely follow rules.

"We're going to sneak into the store after the construction crew leaves," I said to Francesca while dangling my key to the front door. "No one will know."

At 5:00 we had a glass of wine at home, then walked past the permits posted on the façade of the building, laughing while putting on facemasks to protect ourselves from dust. A few passersby gave us momentary stares, then kept going. That's New York.

"Damn," I said, once we got inside, looking at a mess with dust motes in the air and pieces of plaster on the parquet floor that was covered with large plastic drop clothes. "Only the top part of the wall has been removed. At this rate, the project will take longer than expected."

We strode to the wall giggling, then picked at the cracks. Dust fluttered onto my hair turning it from red to gray while I pulled off bigger pieces of plaster.

"*Questo negozio e grande,*" Francesca said, as more sections crashed down.

My bold-patterned heels got caught on the drop cloth. I cursed myself for not wearing sneakers and jeans, dressing well to match Francesca. Big mistake.

A snippet of plaster lodged in the center of my charcoal gray V-neck dress right on top of my grandmother's pearls. Francesca wore the same style dress in her signature red that complemented her full figure and dark, shoulder-length wavy hair. Her oversized red glasses completed the look in a Sophia Loren way. She wore that dress the first time we met in Italy.

It was in the hospital in Prato, outside of Florence. I had visited a new acquaintance, a young man I tried to help after a minor motorcycle accident, except my understanding of Italian was almost nonexistent. I needed an interpreter.

Roberto, a waiter at my hotel who understood English, came to translate. He had already befriended me in the breakfast room. A silly slip-up. You know how it can be when a woman is lost inside herself, alone in a foreign country. Never mind that I call my store *Susanna*'s, the name Roberto called me—his version of Susan. Our almost innocent, thankfully brief moment together has morphed into something clandestine. I learned early in my life that some things must remain private. Thanks to my mother, I can keep a secret.

Soon after Roberto arrived in the hospital lobby, he staggered to the floor with chest pains. Not surprisingly, he asked me to call his wife. I hesitated, wondering how to face this woman after being close to naked with her husband.

Take the high road, my mom had told me. *Life trumps almost naked.*

Instinct took over and I did the right thing. I called her. Francesca was daunting and she knew it. Men followed her with their eyes. Women stood taller in her presence. Me too. I admired her self-assurance and wondered why her husband always brushed my arm with his hand whenever he served my cappuccino.

Though it turned out not to be a heart attack, Francesca was grateful I had helped Roberto. I was thankful she asked no questions. For me, meeting Francesca was a difficult coincidence. I never dreamed we'd go into business together.

"Where did your wife get her dress?" I had said to Roberto during one of our final private moments, before he resumed his psychobabble about life, love and freedom.

"Ah," he said. "You like? She made it—her own design."

"It's sexy while not too low in front. The A-line flatters the hips and the sleeves reach just below the elbow to cover middle-aged arms."

It was far more information than he needed.

"They are beautiful, no?"

"Very beautiful. Where can I buy one?"

"Francesca sells to friends and neighbors. You want? She makes one for you."

"Thanks, but I prefer to try on items before buying. No special order for me," I said, wanting to grab one off the rack someplace.

Soon after, I left Florence to meet my husband in Venice, armed with the concierge's list of places to eat along the Grand Canal near Hotel Danieli where we had booked a room. During the train ride, I decided to erase my escapade by pretending it never happened.

Imagine my shock when Francesca and Roberto showed up at the hotel to give me a package—one of her originals in charcoal gray. She remembered our meeting and had guessed my measurements.

Back in New York I wore that dress almost all the time. My friends wanted something similar. I craved another in black.

"Why not open a boutique featuring all of Francesca's designs?" Kevin had said. "You can use your corporate marketing skills to build your clientele."

The idea felt right. Despite my discomfort, I tracked down Roberto in Florence. He was sure his wife would be thrilled to have her clothes sold in America while he gravitated to the extra money. After a few conversations and consultation with attorneys, we made a deal. Now it was time to forget Roberto and concentrate on the store.

"Maybe we can hurry everything up," I said, grabbing a hammer I found on the floor.

I smacked the wall. Quite a bit collapsed. More dust filled the air and settled on our clothes.

"Here. You take a turn," I said, handing the hammer to Francesca.

She smacked the wall and laughed, "*Facile,* easy," she said.

A large chunk of the wall collapsed at our feet. We both danced backwards a couple of steps to avoid having our toes crushed. Francesca and I peered inside the wall.

"*Dio mio,*" she said, then crossed herself.

Like synchronized ballerinas, we leaned our heads forward. Then there was a familiar ache in my stomach. For a moment, my mind raced back in time, out of my control, to my childhood secret.

"What the hell is that?" I yelled before a scream escaped from my throat. "It's a bone! I think there's a bone in the wall," I said. "Oh my God! Is that a finger? There's a whole hand!"

I stuck my face into the hole. Using the flashlight on my iphone, I could see clearly.

"There's a skeleton in there," I said in a whisper. "It's upside down in a fetal position."

Around its neck was a gold chain dangling a tiny Star of David.

2. Spring, 1954

In the spring of 1954, something big was happening. People were talking about Dr. Salk and his new medicine that might eradicate polio. First, they had to make sure it worked.

"Mommy, my teacher said first and second graders can help get rid of a terrible disease," Leah said while jumping off the burgundy brocade couch under the living room window where she watched people walk along Madison Avenue. "All I have to do is get a shot. Can you sign my permission slip?"

"I von't allow it," Grandma said. "It's a test on humans, on *kinder*, like the Nazis—*Feh*. Nobody knows vat vill happen. It's not for my Leah!"

"Mommy," Leah said, ignoring her grandmother, "my teacher told us hundreds, maybe even thousands of kids will get a shot. All over the country."

"I'm not so sure," her mother, Sarah, said. "You're only seven. It's not good for you to be in some experiment. Come into the kitchen to eat your breakfast."

Leah sat down at the gray Formica table. Using both hands, she poured some milk from a glass bottle into her plastic bowl filled with corn flakes, then fetched a teaspoon.

"Some kids will be given medicine," Leah said, swallowing a spoonful of cereal. "Others will have a shot of nothing."

"Nothing? Is this one of your silly jokes?"

"No, Mommy. I'm not joking. Many of us will not get medicine. It's important to help find a cure. I want the shot."

"You're probably too skinny for this."

"Nobody said anything about being skinny. My teacher told me that if it works, it'll save everyone from polio. Then I can go in a pool this summer."

"What does this vaccination have to do with pools?"

"If there's no more polio, I can't get sick from being in a pool and you'll let me learn how to swim. Please sign my permission slip so I can get a shot with all the other second graders."

"No!" Grandma said in her very loudest voice, stretching her five-foot-two-inch body as high as she could.

"The program sounds important," Leah said, raising her voice to match her grandmother, "maybe even more important than giving my pennies to the Jewish National Fund to plant trees in Israel. I'm not even afraid of the needle, like cousin Rachel."

"Rachel is in fourth grade and too old to participate even if she wants to," Sarah said, then turned to her mother. "Maybe getting the shot is the American thing to do."

"American?" said Grandma, standing taller and using her loudest voice again. "The government is not alvays right. Remember the Russians ven I left. They let the pogroms happen. They let soldiers beat the Jews and do terrible tings to the vomen, to my sister. You must stay avay from anyvone in power."

"It's different here, Mama. You're safe," Sarah said. "We can't always do what you used to do. The old way is not always best. I prefer to keep an open mind to new ideas."

"For vat you need new ideas?"

"To have a more modern life and create a better future for Leah."

"*Feh*," Grandma said again, flicking her wrist.

"Besides, the government isn't running this program," Sarah said while rolling her eyes. "Look at the flyer Leah brought home from school. It says it's the National Foundation for Infantile Paralysis. President Roosevelt started the Foundation almost twenty years ago. You like President Roosevelt."

"I like Roosevelt. I don't vant Leah should have a shot."

"It's the March of Dimes now, Mama. Leah and Rachel both give some of their allowance to them. Even our neighbor's children donate. All six of them. It's part of their learning *tzedakah*, to give to charity. You think that organization is a good idea."

"I don't care vat dey call themselves. She's not getting the shot."

Leah listened and became frightened. Though she turned tongue-tied when she tried to pronounce infantile paralysis, she understood that if she got polio, she might not be able to walk. She could even die. She knew that the boy who lived at the end of the block had to lie in a machine all the time just to breathe. Why did her mother and her grandmother have to scare her? She was already terrified.

"Stop," Leah said, holding her hands to her ears and stamping her feet. "Stop, stop, stop!"

Grandma was so short that when Leah put her face up to her grandmother, their matching dark eyes were almost even.

"I. Want. The. Shot!" Leah shouted, putting her hands on her hips like her grandmother. "And I want to learn how to swim."

"No!" Sarah said.

"Yes! I'm going to get the shot and you can't stop me."

"No. No shot!"

Leah and her mother continued to shout at each other, becoming louder with each sentence until the neighbor, who lived on the second floor just below them, knocked on her ceiling with the handle of a broom.

"That woman is so nice and respectful when she's with her husband," Sarah said, rolling her eyes again. "Banging her broom is not the right way to teach her children good manners. No wonder all six of them are noisy."

"Esther's my favorite friend and she's not noisy. I bet she'll have a shot even though she's only in first grade."

"Maybe, but no shot for you, Leah. I wasn't sure at first. Now, Grandma is making my decision easier."

When it came to Grandma, Mother always argued, then gave in. This time they agreed that Leah could go to class as long as she didn't get the vaccine.

The grown-ups were so distracted they didn't see Leah grab the permission slip and stuff it into the pocket of her dark blue dress. If her parents wouldn't sign, she planned to fill in her mother's name.

The next morning, Grandma padded into the kitchen from her bedroom in the front of the apartment next to the parlor. She was already dressed in her floral housedress topped with one of her many patterned aprons with wide straps over her shoulders that crisscrossed on her back. She raised her arthritic gnarled finger at Leah, telling her "no shot" as her granddaughter ran down the two flights of stairs to the main floor and out the door next to the stores.

Leah waited, twisting her braids that were tied with big white satin bows, until her grandpa came down to take her to school like he did every day. They held hands as he walked and she skipped the few short blocks up Madison Avenue to 81st Street before they reached P.S. 6. On rainy days, if it were really, really bad out, Grandpa splurged on a taxi. No problem today. It was delightfully sunny with a mild spring breeze.

Whenever they walked together, Grandpa would tell her stories about the old country, before he came to America and made lots of money in his tailoring business. Maybe she could get him to sign her permission slip. She almost asked him, then changed her mind, afraid he would call Grandma to see if it were okay. She decided to stick to their usual conversation.

"Grandpa, tell me again. Tell me about the old country."

"Vell, I liked to grow vegetables. Vee had a big garden on the side of the house surrounded by a slatted wood fence. I planted cucumbers and radishes."

"Tell me about the chickens."

"You mean the eggs. Vee had a chicken coop vay behind our house. Such a smell, you vould not believe. It vas so awful I had to hold my breath ven I climbed in to pick up the eggs. I had to be very careful so dey vouldn't break. Some eggs, vee ate. Some vee sold in the open market."

Leah loved her grandpa because he made everything seem easy and good, even building a thatched roof out of mud and straw for their house in Russia. His stories were happy stories. The old place he lived in sounded so different from Grandma's, it made Leah wonder if they came from the same country.

Once inside the school, Leah went right to her classroom and took out the permission slip hidden in her pocket. It was quite crumbled so she spread the paper on her wooden desk and tried to straighten the wrinkles. Next, she printed her mother's name—Sarah. She had only gotten a B in penmanship, probably because she always rushed to finish. This time she wrote slowly so her mom's name would look right. She twisted her braids while waiting for her class to be called into the office where everyone was lining up for the vaccine.

Finally, around 10:00 AM, it was her turn to approach the reception area set-up to check in the students. The woman sitting behind a metal desk glanced through her papers for Leah's name. Nothing.

"I'm sorry. You're not on our list. We can't have you participate unless we have a consent form signed by one of your parents," the lady said.

Leah took out her paper and gave it to the woman who looked at the signature, then asked Leah to wait in a chair on the side of the room. Though the lady smiled, Leah became anxious. Maybe she should have included her mother's last name. Maybe she shouldn't have used a pencil. Maybe her writing was too perfect. For sure, something was wrong.

By 11:00 almost everyone in the first grades and most of the second grades had received shots and returned to their classrooms. Very few children were still lined up so it was eerily quiet as she sat swinging her scrawny legs up and down to keep busy.

Then Leah heard familiar footsteps. Grandma.

Someone had called Leah's home to see if she really had permission and now, Grandma appeared at school to stop her. Leah looked around to see where she could hide. At home, when she was caught doing something mischievous, she always found someplace to sneak into. This office was impossible to escape.

Leah felt thankful that Grandma didn't say anything. Her Russian and Yiddish accent would have been embarrassing. At least she was wearing her good suit instead of her stained apron or a kerchief to cover her hair, dyed to match the brown of her youth, the same color as Leah's.

At times it felt as if Grandma were two different people. The outside Grandma wore pearls and bright red lipstick that made her teeth look very white. That person was strong, even bossy, like now as she yanked Leah by the arm and pulled her into the hallway.

In addition to polio, Leah had been warned about tuberculosis, another disease you could catch from someone else, then cough blood and maybe die. And ever since her school made all the kids kneel down under a desk then cover the back of their necks with their hands, she was afraid of an atomic bomb. These duck-and-cover air-raid practices were kind of like fire drills only scarier because running outside would not bring safety. There were so many bad things sometimes she had trouble concentrating on her lessons.

Right now, she feared Grandma, whose mouth formed a thin line. Her eyebrows were practically touching each other, making her look angry. What could Grandma do?

She never hit. Only her mom or dad could make her miss *Howdy Doody*. Would she take away her Bonomo's Turkish Taffy or candy necklace or her new PEZ dispenser?

The worst would be if Grandma grabbed her King's candy cigarettes that were nestled in her other pocket, the ones that left white powdery stuff on her lips when she sucked on them. In the winter, during outside recess, she looked forward to pretending her breath was smoke. Someday she planned to have real cigarettes, like her daddy, Sol, who smoked so much he smelled like a cigarette.

Everyone called him Solly, though she didn't know why. He always had an unfiltered Camel in his hand or dangling from his lips, even in his drug store when he waited on customers ordering medicine. Sometimes ashes fell on his gray suits, white shirts or red striped ties. When Leah went to his pharmacy, she would watch him brush off the soot then light another cigarette. He did the same at home. Nobody was allowed to yell at Daddy. Grandma screamed at him anyway, telling him not to stink up the place.

Right now, Grandma looked angrier than when she roared at Daddy.

Leah decided to keep quiet. She wanted to be part of the school program. That was her excuse for forging her mother's name, except the shot was exactly what Grandma had told her was forbidden.

"Oh, vey, *Bubala*. Vat did you do?" Grandma said, pointing her gnarled finger. "You make me so angry ven you don't behave. I vorry about you so much. Your moder is in big trouble vit me. Your moder needs to learn how to make you listen."

"Where's Grandpa?" Leah said, ignoring her grandma's words and wishing Grandpa had come to school instead of her.

"Vat do you need vit your grandpa now? You go to your class vitout the shot and forget about this *farkakte* experiment. Next year you get vaccinated—if it's goot. Don't vorry. Dr. Salk is Jewish. He is smart, so I tink his vaccine will help everyone. But using *kinderlach* to see if his medicine works—*Feh!* Such a *mishegas*."

Leah understood enough Yiddish to know her grandmother thought the whole program was crazy. There was no way to change Grandma's mind so she walked to class realizing she would be the only second grader without a Polio Pioneer pin.

3. I Must Find Out Why

Momism: Never force anything.

Francesca and I stood staring at the bones. Not even the sound of breathing could be heard through our masked faces. Just silence. I called my husband and daughter while Francesca made the sign of the cross.

"*Hai la tua catacomba*," she said, crossing herself again.

I paced, looking for other unusual things while Francesca prayed, whispering something about *Santa Maria, Madre di Dio*. About fifteen minutes later, Kevin and Jennifer rushed in.

"I see a skull," Kevin said softly, looking into the hole while putting his arm around me, ever my protector. "A small skull. And teeth. There's a pile of something on the floor under the wrist."

"We should all say a prayer," my daughter said, resting her head on my shoulder. The mother in me understood she felt heartache for the poor soul who had been inside the wall. We all did.

I shifted away from the broken plaster and braced myself against the front door, absorbing the fact that my new rental was not just my professional reincarnation, it could be the scene of a murder.

The skeleton was small. Was it a child? My mind raced back in time, out of my control, to the secret I'd kept for so very long. I pressed at the familiar ache in my stomach.

There's no connection between the skeleton and you, Mom said, in an angry, clipped voice. *This has nothing to do with our family.*

With great effort, I refocused. Should we notify the police and admit we were inside the store after hours or should we let the workers find the skeleton in the morning?

"Is it an offense to find a body and not report it?" I said to Kevin as he brushed dust off his navy blazer.

"Why do that?"

"We don't belong here," I said. "Maybe we'd get fined."

"Probably a small fine. What's your real reason for wanting to leave?"

"Not to get involved," I said, recognizing how terrible that sounded.

"Susan, it's your store so on some level, we're already involved. Our responsibility is to bring in the authorities. Now!"

I nodded yes, appreciating Kevin who always opts to do the right thing.

"I bet the person was very young," I said, feeling goose bumps appear on my arms. "I keep wondering if it was already dead when placed inside the wall or did the wall form a trap?"

Before I could dwell on this any longer, Francesca tapped me on the shoulder. "We call police?" she said.

"Yes. We're about to go public," I said, pointing to Jennifer who I had asked to dial 911.

While we waited for the cops, my mind raced with more questions. What impact would this news have on my boutique? I know it doesn't sound kind, but the place is my business. As a publicist, what spin would I have to take and how could I sell clothes under such a cloud?

"Mom," Jennifer said, jolting me out of my private thoughts. "I wonder who lives in the above apartments. Maybe they know who this was. And who owned the store before you?"

"The landlord would know those answers. Since there are only bones left, the tragedy must have occurred a long time ago. I don't think the same people would still be here."

Jennifer walked over to the hole again. "I can see the entire skeleton and there are pieces of burgundy fabric that looks like a wintry dress or coat," she said.

"Maybe you should get out of your lease," Kevin said. "We can afford to step away."

"It took months to find this place."

Kevin encircled me with his arms again. Despite my strength, I let him look after me. It's one of our unspoken marital understandings. It's nice to know he has my back.

"We've already spent money on lawyers and accountants as well as making endless calls to real estate agents to get the place. I don't want to do this again," I said, before sirens drowned out my voice.

Two flashing cop cars pulled up outside the building, stopping under a no parking sign. A crowd began to gather on the sidewalk, peering through the windows to see what happened, taking pictures on cell phones.

After a quick hello, one young officer asked Kevin who's in charge, then did an appreciative double take when he saw Francesca.

"We got a call about a skeleton. What's going on? Who's in charge?" a second, female officer said.

"I am. I'm the new tenant, turning these two stores into one. That's how we found the bones," I said, walking over to the skeleton.

The young cop, opting to walk with Francesca, followed. The female officer stayed with me. She was tall. Add her hat, gun and dark blue uniform and she inspired a mixture of confidence with a don't-mess-with-me fear. Her penetrating eye contact took away any sense of influence I thought I had.

To fight a new feeling of helplessness, I stepped forward. Jennifer tugged on my elbow trying to pull me away. Too late. I had already claimed responsibility for the gathering and now felt flush. A rash that starts on my neck and works its way up through my cheeks is a new development since my return from Italy a few months ago. It appears whenever I get nervous. Though I had nothing to do with this bizarre finding, I felt uneasy, especially when the officer took down my contact info.

I felt Francesca watching, opening then closing her mouth. She had stopped crossing herself and was smiling at the cop who seemed glued to her side. The skeleton situation was so obvious that despite the language barrier, she could figure it out and was openly flirting. We must have looked odd, two middle-aged women wearing matching dresses, or maybe nobody noticed.

"Didn't your construction company tell you this site is off limits?" the female officer said to me. She didn't smile. I wondered if that were part of her training. I looked out the front window and saw two other officers putting up crime scene tape and realized my construction crew would not be allowed to work here for a while. I also saw photographers snapping shots.

"Do you think there are more bones in the other walls," I said, starting to babble.

The cops ignored my question, telling all of us to stand aside.

"It looks like someone sealed the body inside the wall. That's no accident," I said, continuing to chatter nervously, hoping she would loosen up.

"Until we have facts, I really can't comment. Can you give me the name and number of the landlord?" she said, before walking over to her partner near the front door. Then she returned, this time engaging Kevin.

"Aren't you Doctor Kendall?" she said. "I saw you on the cover of *New York* magazine." Kevin nodded.

"Susan is my wife, the owner of this new boutique," he said, trying to redirect the cop to me. It didn't work. He became her go-to person, while I stood in his shadow.

"The body must have been inside the wall for years because there's no blood or skin or organs left," I said to Jennifer as I inched as close as I could to Kevin, trying to hear what they said. Jennifer pulled me away again.

"Mom, why not let the police do their work?"

"But it's my store."

"They'll get to you. Give them a chance to do it their way."

Part of me agreed. I wanted to let go, stick to my business. I certainly had enough to keep me busy. I didn't want to care about the skeleton, but I did. Then I didn't, flip-flopping all within one minute. This was not my normal decisive way of approaching a situation.

"I can't," I said. "There are people out there who need to know what happened to their relative. Can you imagine all the years they agonized over this loss? Perhaps my tenacity can be of some help."

People can get over losses without your support, my mother said. I chose to ignore her.

"Finding a skeleton in the wall is a grisly coincidence," Jennifer said. "You should stay out of it."

"I don't believe in coincidences. This is not just a cold case. It's a tragedy for a family. Maybe I'm supposed to help."

"The cops won't work with you. If you insist on being your usual stubborn self, you should find a private detective to work with."

"A detective!"

"Yes, and I know the perfect person."

"You do. Who?"

"Sean's girlfriend's father."

"What? What are you saying?"

"Sean has a new girlfriend. Her dad is a detective."

"Your brother never mentioned he's in a relationship." I felt like I'd been punched in the stomach. "I can't believe he didn't tell me."

"Aren't you glad Sean found someone who makes him happy? She's in medical school with him. They have classes together. Her dad is exactly the right person for you to talk to," she said, kicking dust off her new sneakers.

"You and your brother went to the top private schools in Manhattan, then graduated Ivy League. Obviously, if this girl's dad is a detective, she's from a different type of family."

"Why does that matter?"

"It doesn't matter. Not really, it's just not what I expected. What does her mother do?"

"She's a nurse."

My daughter's disapproving look made me uncomfortable.

"I'm surprised at you, Mom. What about your lectures regarding being politically correct?"

"You mean everyone is created equal. We all deserve a good education, a chance for a better life," I said. "I still believe it."

"I feel a huge rationalization coming on," Jennifer said. "And it won't be pretty."

"Okay, okay, I know I can continue expounding about how I mentor assistants and donate money to charities, except we're talking about my son and his future. I believe most parents want their grown children to bring home someone from a similar background. The more similar, the better chance they have for a happy, successful relationship."

"Mom, you sound like a hypocrite. You don't even know this girl. Whomever Sean chooses won't be your clone. It's out of your control. You can't arrange his marriage."

"Marriage! It's that serious?" I said as my rash started up my neck and on to my cheek.

"Kevin," I said, a bit too loudly. "Kevin, you have to come here."

Francesca stepped aside, not understanding what was going on.

"Sean has a serious girlfriend," I said.

"Yes, he told me."

"You already know!"

"I shouldn't have said anything," Jennifer said. "Please wait until he's ready to share his news, then act surprised."

I tried to push down the rage I felt, then asked the cops when we could leave. I didn't mention losing money if the opening got delayed. I didn't say anything about the mystery pulling me in to find the victim's family. There was no time to think about that right now. Francesca and I were due at an early evening photo shoot for our ads. That's why we were dressed alike.

Most of all, I needed to call my son.

4. Summer, 1954

"Stop wiggling," Leah's mother said while holding up one of her daughter's summer dresses to see if it was still long enough. "It's hard to pack while you're darting here and there. You're making me crazy."

Leah settled on the single bed with her dark hair wrapped around the cardboard centers of toilet paper rolls so she would have nice curls framing her face. She was so excited to be going to the country she couldn't keep still.

"Mommy, can I stay with cousin Rachel in her cottage?" Leah said, leaping up, careful not to wrinkle the new pink floral bedspread her mother had bought using the money she saved sewing some of the clothes for Leah and herself. "I want to do everything Rachel does."

Rachel's parents, Karl and Dina, owned The Lakeside Hotel in the Catskills. Uncle Karl only came up on weekends because he needed to work in his New York law office during the week. Dina spent the whole season with Grandma and Grandpa in a cottage on the grounds so all the hotel rooms could be available for guests.

Every night, Dina recorded each penny they paid for food, the wait-staff and cleaning crew, entertainers, even the cost of replacing a single light bulb, a box of Band-Aids or a bigger item like an Adirondack chair.

Sometimes she invited Rachel and Leah to watch, so they would learn about expenses, but Leah already knew to write things down. She watched her mother do the same thing at home and she knew Grandma did it for Grandpa in his tailoring shop.

"You can stay with her if you promise not to wander off on your own like you did last year," Sarah said. "You have to follow the rules, just like Rachel. *All* the rules."

"What if I get curious?"

"No exploring, *Bubala*. I don't want you to get lost in the woods."

"I'm afraid of the forest," Leah said.

"Since when?"

"Only kidding, Mommy. If Rachel comes with me, can we go to the woods together?"

"No, and your jokes aren't funny. You always do what you want, just like my sister when we were growing up. She was always off somewhere, getting into trouble until Grandma found her. You even look like Aunt Dina," Leah's mother said, with a smile.

"And everyone says Rachel looks like you, Mommy. She has your blue eyes and blonde hair. Grandma thinks we were switched at birth."

"You know that's impossible. Rachel is two years older."

"I want to be like her. Can I do whatever she does during our vacation?"

"What exactly do you want to do?"

"Learn how to swim. Please can I learn how to swim this time? Rachel said she can teach me."

"*Bubala*," her mother said, "you know you aren't allowed in public pools. It's too dangerous. You can catch something really bad."

"Like what?"

"Like polio, that's what. We already went over this when you wanted to get the shot at school."

"Mommy, if I can't swim in the pool, can I go in the lake? Please, please, please can I go in the lake?"

"The lake water will be icy, even though it's August. You'll catch a cold."

Leah kept quiet as she often did when planning to misbehave. She knew how to get her way. Then she thought about her grandparents who lived with them in the winter but stayed with Aunt Dina in the country for the summer. Any sneaking would have to be done while Grandma was busy helping Aunt Dina in the hotel kitchen, wearing her housedress and wiping her hands on her stained apron while hollering at the busboys to clear the plates and the waiters to hurry up and serve the guests as fast as possible.

Grandma was home in New York with them this week. She had to go to a doctor for pains in her chest. With new medicine, she was ready to travel back up to the country. While Leah packed, Grandma came into her room and sat on the bed next to Leah's valise. Instead of her usual housecoat, Grandma was dressed in her outside clothes wearing a charcoal gray suit, pearls and her gold brooch, eager to leave the house to go upstate.

"Leah," Grandma said. "I brought for you a potato knish. Eat. *Ess*."

Leah remembered last summer when Grandma followed her with food, complaining she was too skinny. Grandma was loud. Everyone nearby could hear her and look at Leah to decide if she really was so thin. She knew guests were watching when she turned around and faced a hardboiled egg balanced on a spoon or a paper cup full of fruit or corn flakes. It was always something healthy, never Jolly Time popcorn or Hershey's milk chocolate. If Leah heard Grandma coming, sometimes she ran the other way to hide. Here, in her bedroom, there was no escape.

"Leah," Grandma said, while pushing the potato knish close to her lips, "remember, never kiss or hug anyvone at the hotel, not even cousin Rachel or Aunt Dina or Uncle Karl."

"Why?" Leah said, taking the smallest bite possible. The knish was cold and dried out. She hoped bits wouldn't get stuck in her throat. "Why can't I hug anybody?"

"Because dere's a terrible disease you can catch."

"I know all about polio," Leah said.

"That too, but dis time I am talking about Tuberculosis. It vill make you cough and maybe vorse. Kissing anyvone, even relatives, is how you can catch TB."

Leah wished Mommy and Grandma would talk about happy stuff, like buying a television so she could see *Howdy Doody* at home instead of downstairs in the neighbor's apartment. She especially liked watching Clarabell the Clown and the Peanut Gallery.

Whenever she joined them, the neighbor's children sat in two rows in front of their new RCA set. Leah was in the second row, happy to be there though sometimes she had trouble seeing the small screen over the other kids' heads. She also had to put up with

Esther's older sister, Malka, who was mean to her. Still, it was better than no TV until her parents bought one of their own.

All the grown-ups in her family said home was the best place to be so after school, she often stayed in their apartment. Sometimes she practiced with her hula-hoop in the living room, careful not to knock over the crystal candy dish filled with nuts or the fancy bowl on the coffee table. Esther often came upstairs and copied Leah, doing whatever games her older neighbor made up. But not today. Today, they were leaving for the country. It was supposed to be safer there, yet all her mother and grandmother talked about were bad things.

"Grandma, why are you always worried?" Leah said.

"Leave Grandma alone," Sarah said. "Just help me pack."

"It's okay, *Bubala*," Grandma said. "I vorry because of the old country."

"What happened?" Leah knew she would only get half an answer like every other time she asked her grandparents about their past life.

"Ve had sickness, too, but mostly I hid from bad people. I vas small and good at hiding."

"Why did you hide?"

"Bad soldiers hated Jews. The men came on horses and beat people. My older sister and her friend were taken to the woods. My sister always cried after she came back. We never saw her friend again."

"What happened?"

"I don't vant to talk about dose times. Just know, it was so bad, we left."

"Leah, people don't flee their homeland if life is good," Mommy said.

Though she had heard this before, hearing parts of what was so awful made Leah anxious. She fidgeted, then gave Grandma a hug even though it wasn't allowed.

"Vee got lucky," Grandma said, turning her face away and removing Leah's arms from around her waist. "Vee ran avay. Later we came here, to America. It vas in 1904, vay before you ver born. I vas 15 years old."

"Tell me again, where is the old country?" Leah said.

She already knew that her relatives came from someplace in the U.S.S.R., a part of Russia called Belarus, or maybe they said the Ukraine. She wasn't sure and since nobody showed her a map, the fancy names seemed as far away as the moon. She didn't understand why Grandma worried so much now that she didn't have to hide.

"Who'd you come with?" Leah said, hoping Grandma would add something new.

"With my thirteen brothers and sisters, vee came," Grandma said, "but not at the same time. The first to come here sent money for the next von so vee vere on different ships. Oy, vee got so sick in the bottom of the boat. Grandpa, too. He and his brothers and sisters, all nine of them, started to come over in 1906. Dey also came to America separately. Vee couldn't bring lots of tings, not even as many clothes like you are packing for your vacation."

"And then what happened?" Leah said, while putting her favorite black patent leather Mary Jane shoes in her bag.

"Vee all tried to get educated and find vork. The best were Friday nights. Each family would gather every veek for Shabbat dinner. That helped us stay together."

"Like we do with Aunt Dina, Uncle Karl and cousin Rachel on Friday nights."

"Yes. And you vill do the same when you grow up and have your own family."

Leah said nothing, trying to imagine so many years in the future.

"After everyone married and had children," Grandma said, "nobody moved far avay like to California or Florida. Vee all stuck together on the Lower East Side or uptown in Manhattan or the Bronx. Later, the more brave vons, dey left the neighborhood and moved to Queens or Long Island. The vons vit the most money," she said, while raising an index finger in the air, "dey vent to Vestchester. We could always drive to visit for a day."

"Mama," Sarah said. "Leah's only seven. She has no idea what you are saying."

"What about your dinners?" Leah said, promising herself that when she grew up, she would see all these places. Maybe if she had money, she would move to Vestchester, wherever that was.

"Each family still met once a veek, except we switched to Sunday lunch."

Now, Grandma whispered. "Ven vee came here, first vee stopped at Ellis Island. Oy vee vere scared. One relative coughed so much, the government put a chalk mark on her coat. Vee erased it right avay. Vee thought she had tuberculosis and would not be allowed in the country."

Leah was tired of illnesses. She wanted to hear a cheerful story.

"Tell me how you met Grandpa," she said, while packing two more dresses, the ones Mother had bought on sale at Alexander's.

"Vee met at a street party on the Lower East Side of Manhattan. I vas 18. He vas von year older. There were policemen on horses. They reminded me of the old country, of the Cossacks. Ven I saw dem, I fainted. Your grandpa helped me up. Ven I opened my eyes, I saw the most handsome man. He called me his *shayna maidel,* his pretty girl. He still calls me his *shayna maidel.*"

Leah had seen policemen on horses and nobody had fainted. Perhaps that only happened at street events. She had never seen a party in the street. Maybe there were no parties anymore or maybe there were none uptown on Madison Avenue. She imagined the events had music and food and must have been lots of fun.

"More and more family came over on the ships and started having families of their own. Soon enough, your mother had 51 first cousins," Grandma said. "51! Too many for weekly dinners so dey started a cousin's club to meet every month. This August, the meeting vill be at Aunt Dina's hotel. Too bad it is in a part of the Catskills vere the German Jews go. *Feh!*"

"What's wrong with German Jews?" Leah asked.

"Dey think dey are better den us. I don't know vhy Dina bought a hotel dere. Vee like to be in another section with other Russian Jews. Vee call it the Borscht Belt."

"Why do you call it the Borsht Belt?"

"Because Russians like to eat borsht."

Leah was totally confused. She knew that borscht was red beet soup and of course, she knew what a belt was. How people could gather at hotels in a Borscht Belt remained so far beyond her imagination that she decided to ignore it. The important thing was the family going to the mountains, away from the heat and disease of the city.

She would miss Esther, but not Malka who often came upstairs to fetch her little sister when they played together.

The last dress Leah packed was her pink and white one with the biggest pockets. Grandma had sewed it for her out of an old tablecloth. Leah hated wearing clothes made from curtains and discarded brocade fabric. It made her look odd among the other girls at school. She also hated the stitching lessons Grandma insisted on giving her, telling her she must learn how to sew and may she never need to, whatever that meant.

"You have enough dresses," her mother said, hanging the pink dress back in the closet. "Besides, I thought you liked your other outfits better."

"I do, but I also have to have this one."

"Vey do you need dis dress?"

"Because it has big pockets," Leah said

"*Bubala,* for vat you need pockets?"

"Things."

"Let her take it," Grandma said. "Von more. Vat difference does it make?"

"Thank you, Grandma," Leah said, with a shrug of her shoulders, wishing she could hug her grandmother.

"First she needs to finish her knish."

Before anyone asked Leah more questions, they heard a car beeping downstairs.

"I hear Solly," Grandma said, getting up and straightening her skirt.

Sure enough, Leah's father had pulled up outside and was honking the horn of their old Chevrolet Bel Aire hard top, the one he bought after Grandma taught him how to drive. Everyone said Grandma was very modern. That was before Leah was born, when her grandparents had earned a lot of money in their tailoring shop.

By now, Daddy was inside and in such a rush he raced upstairs to get the luggage without bothering to change out of his suit.

"Daddy's here! Daddy's here," Leah said, while hopping up and down.

"Leah, we're leaving. Stop jumping around and finish packing," her mother said. "And you don't need to take a bathing suit so put it back in your drawer."

When her mother turned around, Leah rolled her pink-dotted bathing suit and cap inside a shirt and pushed it to the bottom of her bag.

"Okay, Mommy," she said, with a not-so-innocent smile. "May I leave my hula hoop for Esther to use? I can put it by her door on the way out."

"That's very nice. And be sure to take your cheese box full of crayons and your coloring pad."

5. A Media Circus

Momism: Understand the other side.

"Honey," Kevin said, from his office, three days after we discovered the skeleton. "I'm just calling to let you know the same photos we saw on TV last night appeared this morning in *The Post, The New York Times*, and a stack of other papers. Most likely they're also online."

"Which pictures did they print?"

"One of the skeleton in a fetal position nestled in the wall. You can see the gold chain with a tiny Star of David around its neck."

"Is that all?" I said, hoping my face was not included.

"Well," he said, delaying his response. "Some newspapers carried a second shot, a new one of you staring at the hole from a side angle. Your mouth is wide open as if you were visiting the dentist."

"One of the photographers looking through the store window must have taken it. I saw it on TV this morning. Not very flattering. Does the article mention *Susanna's*?"

"Yes, that's the good news. The papers included the address of the store. On the down side, they mention both our names. It'll be easy for anyone to find us. Don't be surprised if there are journalists outside our apartment building. I already received a few calls from reporters."

"Oh Kev, I feel terrible. My project is interrupting your work. People are also commenting on social media. Everyone has an opinion about what happened. Even the doorman and neighbors stopped me to ask questions. I loathe losing my privacy. Don't laugh. I think I'm going to go out with a disguise."

"Not so sure that will help, but have fun with it," he said, laughing. "Good thing Francesca flew home or you'd both be incognito."

I smiled though Kevin couldn't see me. Maybe it was the relief I felt since yesterday when Francesca had gotten into a taxi to go to the airport. Her leaving was one less thing to worry about and finally, I could stop thinking about Roberto. Of course, I couldn't tell Kevin any of my feelings and that made me sad. My secret seemed to grow more arms than an octopus, each one stretching out to separate me from my husband. Maybe I should let him know what I did in Florence and, more important, what I didn't do. Not today, though. Not yet.

I hung up and shuffled down the long hall from our kitchen to the master bedroom. Since apartments in New York don't have tremendous storage space, after Jessica married, we transformed her bedroom into two closets. The smaller one held 25 pairs of jeans if you count jeggings, denim, whites and blacks. Then there was a row of workout clothes and casual outfits.

Max followed me into the larger closet as I surveyed the top shelf of hats lined up in between recessed lights in the ceiling. The plush white carpeting and full-length mirror gave my private space an airy feeling despite an embarrassing number of blouses hanging above a row of pants on one wall. Dresses and suits were on another. I hoped to duplicate this atmosphere in the store.

My camouflage of choice was a black hat whose wide brim nearly reached my eyes which I covered with oversized black sunglasses. I wished I looked half as glamorous as Audrey Hepburn. I knew the hat was not a real disguise and bones found in a posh neighborhood on the Upper East Side were way too juicy to be ignored. For sure, the press would not leave me alone now that my name and pictures of me were splashed all over the papers.

In my old professional world, I was more than willing to help each journalist land a good story, while my job always kept me in the background. The spotlight belonged to others. I liked it that way. At the same time, publicity for the boutique would be wonderful.

The minute I stepped out, a young woman started to walk with me. She was dressed in a short-sleeved black dress and sneakers, much like my daughter would wear on her commute to work. A small shoulder bag was draped across her chest. She also carried an oversized tote bag that bulged with papers sticking out on top.

"Good morning," she said, with a smile as wide as mine. "I'm Dottie from the *New York Post*. Can you tell me how you discovered the skeleton in your wall? Do you suppose the person in the wall was super rich like the people who now live in this area? And what's with the Star of David? Was it a hate crime?"

Before I had time to answer, she asked more questions.

"The police sent out a press release asking for information. Have they interviewed you? What did you tell them?"

She continued this barrage while we walked in tandem over to Fairway on East 86th Street. Thank goodness today I had switched from Manolo Blahnik heels to ballet flats. The quicker I walked, the quicker she followed. When I hurried across the street to make the light, she ran by my side. This was the first reporter who tried to get me to make some comment. I realized that dealing with only one person right now, with one set of questions, was a break.

Once inside Fairway, it was obvious that Dottie wouldn't leave me alone. While she selected cherries and I touched the avocados, I decided to make her feel like a buddy. I managed a smile, then asked the usual questions.

"How long have you worked at the Post? Do you like your beat? What's the best assignment you've had? What are your career goals? Maybe I can help with details for this story."

Every answer Dottie gave led to another question as we continued to get to know each other until we left the store each carrying a small bag of produce.

"May I buy you a manicure?" I said, walking toward Blooming Nails over on 89th and Lex.

"Thanks, I'm good. I couldn't accept even if I wanted to. Tell me something. Anything. Finding bones means whatever happened was long ago, so I checked if there are other cold cases in the neighborhood. Nothing."

I shrugged my shoulders.

"What did the police tell you?" she said.

"The police? Zilch. They sound as stilted as you see in the movies. Did you get any information out of them?"

"Just the press release. I think the location of your boutique and the Star of David makes the story more interesting. How do you feel about setting up business in a possible crime scene? It's the antithesis of high fashion in a posh area."

"I keep asking myself the same question. It's a hell of a mess and will delay my opening. Oh, is this conversation off the record?" I said, watching her write something in her notepad. Maybe if I kept quiet, I could keep my name out of future stories. Too bad keeping quiet is not my nature.

"Off the record? Why do you care? You didn't do anything wrong. Tell you what, work with me and I'll give your boutique a good plug."

"You've got yourself a deal, but with no information to share just yet, this feels as solid as Jell-O. Is there some other less factual angle we can use?"

"There's always another angle. How about your personal take? Don't you think it's a bit creepy? Disturbing at the very least?" Dottie said.

"Disturbing and sad."

She nodded.

"What do you plan to do next?"

"Next? I plan to complete renovations and open my store. What would you do?"

"I'm a reporter," she said, laughing. "I'd find out all I could about the skeleton and run with the story. Maybe unearth facts the cops might miss. There's got to be some family out there who's been wondering all these years what happened to their loved one."

Her words hit home. Finding the truth was beginning to grow on me. I was already thinking of the skeleton as mine.

"I have kids," I said. "I can't imagine what it would be like if one disappeared and we never learned what happened."

She nodded again.

"I'm practical so I hear how irrational this might sound, but discovering bones in *my* boutique feels like a sign telling me to find the family."

"And you think you can do this?" Dottie said.

"At least I can try."

I didn't tell her that it might be more gratifying than simply selling high-fashion clothes. Nor did I mention my own childhood secret that plagued me and made me want to help the family. Instead, I promised myself I'd call the detective Jennifer had mentioned.

"What about your shop? When will you open?" Dottie said.

Finally, a question that could give me positive publicity. I stopped, removed my sunglasses and faced her as other pedestrians, some walking dogs, brushed by.

"As soon as possible. It's called *Susanna's*. S-U-S-A-N-N-A apostrophe S. Please spell it right if you're going to mention it. And I hope you do."

Don't be condescending, Susan, my mother said. *She's just trying to do her job.*

"You give me anything you find," Dottie said, "and like I said, I'll plug your store. Your name is Susan. Why do you call your place *Susanna's*?"

"Good question. My designer is Italian," I said, with a smile my mother would like, showing off my bleached-white teeth. "Her husband calls me Susanna with the letter s in the middle pronounced like a z. I hope it implies that we carry Italian styles."

"Your designer's husband has a pet name for you?"

"Well, yes. I mean no," I said, flustered, quickly putting my glasses back on, hoping to hide whatever expression I had.

Dottie looked down while taking notes. Maybe she smiled. The shadow from my hat and my dark glasses stopped me from being sure. While I tried to loosen up, to enjoy the warm spring breeze that ruffled the skirt of my black linen dress, she switched back to the crime scene.

"And the skeleton? Do you think it will bring in customers or keep them away?"

Before I could answer, another reporter appeared along with a photographer. He snapped my photo. The journalists seemed to know one another and chatted softly.

The new reporter showed me the article Kevin had mentioned. I saw that my husband had omitted sharing the caption where I was listed as the new shop owner and wife of noted plastic surgeon, Kevin Kendall. Was that relevant? Even concerning my skeleton, I was shifted into his shadow again. I knew it was petty, but couldn't stop myself from calling Kevin to complain.

When he answered, he seemed frazzled. I felt awful causing him trouble.

"I'm getting tons of calls," he said. "Some are from reporters. That's not as bad as the others, people claiming the bones belong to someone in their family. It's upsetting to learn there are so many missing persons.

Maybe because the article said the remains were small, inquiries are mostly about children. One man insisted it was his dog."

"I want to know who all these people are," I said.

"I figured you would. The police asked us to keep a list of all callers and their phone numbers. I have a copy for you."

After I hung up, I rejoined Dottie to walk south on Madison Avenue toward the store. When we got closer, we spotted cameras set up with crews filming the building. Too bad my boutique sign was not up yet. Then someone yelled, "There she is!"

Four cameras turned toward me. With Dottie still at my side, we ducked under the police barricade and entered the store. The place was a mess. No one saw us enter at first and we instinctively stayed near the door to watch. There were uniformed police looking at walls, dusting for fingerprints, taking pictures and using what looked like hi-tech devices to check the other walls for additional bones.

They moved quickly. At least my workers would soon be allowed back in. Then our attention was drawn outside where someone was speaking into a microphone.

"Want another free plug?" asked Dottie, nudging my elbow and gesturing with her head. "There's your shot."

She was right. Steeling myself, I gathered my talking points in my mind, marched outside and grabbed the mike from an astonished assistant who'd been testing it. I faced the cameras.

"Thank you all for coming," I said, as if I had invited them to this impromptu press conference. "While I envisioned beautiful Italian dresses for mature, chic women, I find myself enmeshed in a chilling mystery. I'm sure you can imagine the complicated feelings my designer and I had when we discovered the bones. It was gruesome to see a finger, a wrist and an arm."

At first, these were just words. The minute I uttered them I felt how macabre the situation was. My face flushed. Dottie nodded and smiled. I took that as encouragement to continue. The TV crews surrounded me, shoving their microphones into my face, forcing me to lean back so I wasn't hit in the mouth.

"What did you do after you discovered the skeleton?" a sweaty man in an ill-fitting suit yelled out.

"I did what anyone would do. I called the police."

"Do you know the dead person?"

"No, I—"

"What's your role in finding this?"

One question came after another. The press of bodies got closer.

"What do the police say?"

I shrugged my shoulders and shook my head.

"Will you go public with any findings?"

"Of course. I am as curious and caring as you. I'm sure the police will keep you abreast of the developing situation."

It was time to try to get a plug in for the store, though it felt tactless in comparison to the severity of the situation. Still, I carried on.

"I know this is a grave situation and have great faith that the police will solve it in time. Meanwhile, I'd like to invite all of you back to Susanna's, that's 'S U S A N N A's with an apostrophe 's,' when the boutique's construction is complete."

The door to the shop opened and the police filed out. I thanked Dottie quickly for her time and slipped back into the store amongst the renewed frenzy of questions, this time, thankfully directed at the departing police.

The rest of the morning was chaos. People stopped in front of the store to stare through the windows. By the afternoon, it was quiet. I craved a drink and some down time. When Kevin called, it was easy for him to convince me to meet for an early dinner.

I closed immediately. Outside I turned left to walk down to 74th Street then took another left to Third Avenue where I saw Kevin entering the TBar Steakhouse.

"I'm starving, hon," he said when I caught up. "Let's order right away. You want to start with your favorite Caesar Salad?"

"Sounds perfect."

"I'll stick to my usual Iceberg Wedge. Your hat looks lovely. Fool anyone?"

"Reporters found me right away," I said, leaning back in my chair, slipping off my shoe and massaging my toes along Kevin's leg under the table. He gave a contented sigh.

We splurged on a bottle of Barolo then shared a rare, and I do mean rare, Black Angus Porterhouse for two. The steak was so good I put down my knife and fork, picked up the bone and chewed off the remaining scraps, confidant that nobody could see me since our table was in the rear.

"Want to share the warm Apple Crisp with ice cream?" Kevin said.

"Full," I said, patting my tummy. "For sure I'll regret this meal tomorrow."

The next day, *The Post* carried a new photo of me. My face was recognizable, though my mouth was concealed by the bone and my cheeks were covered with bits of meat and grease. At least the article quoted all my comments and good intentions.

The caption read: *Bone Lady Takes on Cold-Case Skeleton.*

6. Summer, 1954

Leah woke up first. She crept over to Rachel's bed and tickled her cousin's neck. It was just getting light out, a perfect time to do whatever they wanted to do under their parents' radar. Since they were sharing a room, it was easy to whisper and not disturb the adults. The bare wooden floor felt cold on their feet. They didn't care.

"Help me make my bed," Leah said. "The mattress is too heavy for me to do those corners you showed me."

"No problem," Rachel said as she tucked the top sheet in. "My mother's so fussy we have to do it right or she'll make us come back and do it again."

As soon as they finished, the girls tiptoed to the kitchen, gulped down some corn flakes and milk, then rinsed their bowls before replacing them in the wooden cupboard that had been painted shades of sage so many times it was chipping. Leah climbed up on the counter to reach the proper shelf as Rachel grabbed a leftover cookie.

"Are you sure nobody can see us?" Leah said, while moving the lace curtain just enough to peak out the window.

"Nobody's awake yet, except the kitchen staff setting up for breakfast. The pool is on the other side of the dining room so I think we'll be okay."

Somehow, they managed to contain their giggles until they slipped out the door. They raced across the porch and down the crooked wooden steps careful to grasp the wooden railing gently to avoid splinters.

"It feels like you're the older cousin," Rachel said. "You always have the best ideas. Sometimes they're scary. I don't know why I listen to you."

"Oh, don't be such a worrywart. You're worse than Grandma. Come on. You promised to teach me to swim. Now's my chance."

"I know, but there's no lifeguard this early. What if you can't do it? It'll be my fault if you drown."

"It can't be your fault if it's my idea."

"Who told you that?"

"Nobody. It just makes sense. Besides, I got a lifeguard to come."

"You did! Which one? How did you do it?"

"Only kidding."

"I hate your jokes."

"I'm not going to drown, and that's no joke."

"What makes you so sure?"

"I'm going to stay by the side so I can grab on to the edge. I won't leave the shallow end where I can stand."

"One of the lifeguards said you can drown in a little bit of water."

"I'll keep my mouth above the water so I'll be safe."

"If you don't put your face in the water, how can you learn to swim?"

"Maybe I'll need more than one lesson. At least I can start today."

When they reached the shallow end of the pool, Rachel slipped off her shoes and blue dress. She folded it carefully before placing it on a chair. Leah had already stepped out of her loose pink cover-up letting it fall on the thick cement that separated the swim area from the grass. First they held onto each other for balance so they could dip their toes in and out. Next, they sat down and dangled their feet. There were no towels in sight.

"Oh my God, the water is sooo cold," Leah said.

"Believe me, if you think this is cold, you'll never go into the lake. I told you last year, the water comes down from the mountains then flows through the lake into a stream. Remember?"

"I remember. I told that to my mother because I thought she would allow me to go in the lake."

"What did she say?"

"No. That's all she ever says when I want to do something."

"Once, I fell out of a canoe and it was freezing," Rachel said.

"What happened?"

"I climbed back in, silly. I'm still here, right?"

"Can you die from the cold?"

"I guess. I didn't, so maybe it isn't as cold as I think."

By now, their feet had acclimated to the temperature. Rachel was the first to jump in, instantly submerging to the bottom of her armpits. Leah followed. The water covered her shoulders even though she was standing on her toes, trying to be taller. She held onto the edge so tightly the skin on her knuckles stretched thin.

"I'm not sure how to teach you," Rachel said. "I watched the lifeguards give a lesson once. They told the kids to make the water a friend and pretend they were resting in bed."

"I don't know about that," Leah said. "Can I start with kicking while I hold on? Maybe it'll get warmer."

The girls moved their legs, splashing and giggling. They were having such a good time they forgot to be quiet until someone yanked Leah by her scrawny arm and pulled her out of the pool.

"What do you think you're doing?" her mother yelled. "Do you want to get polio? Do you want to drown? I told you not to go into the pool. Why can't you ever listen?"

"I want to learn how to swim," Leah said, rubbing her knee which she just scraped on the cement that had weeds poking up from the cracks. "Everyone else my age can swim and they don't have polio. Why am I the only one who can't do anything?"

"Wait until Grandma finds out," her mother said. "She'll be angry with me, not you. She'll tell me, again, that in the old country, children obeyed their parents. You don't obey me so I must be a bad parent. You, my little lady, are getting me in trouble."

"I can still sleep in the bungalow with Rachel, right?"

"Absolutely not. You will sleep in the hotel in our room where we can watch you. No more slipping out before the hotel breakfast. No more swimming. It's a good thing one of the waiters saw kids in the pool on his way to the kitchen. 'Kids are in the pool' was blasted over the loudspeaker. I knew it was you."

"Can I learn to swim in the lake? The water keeps moving from the mountains down to the stream so I bet the polio doesn't get stuck there."

"No," her mother said, raising her left eyebrow and grabbing Leah, pulling her toward the hotel.

Rachel was left on her own wondering if she were also in trouble, not with her mother, but with her grandmother. If she got yelled at, she would remind Grandma that her mom allowed her to swim in both the lake and the pool. She decided to go to the kitchen to find her grandmother and tell her what happened. Maybe then she could grab another cookie or a fresh bun. Since Leah couldn't stay in the bungalow anymore, she felt as if she were also being punished. She would have to wait until lunchtime to meet up with her cousin again.

"Vat's da matter, Rachel? You look unhappy," Grandma said while taking out some rolls from the giant oven.

"Leah can't stay in our bungalow anymore," Rachel said.

"Vhy? Dere must be a reason. She must have done someting wrong."

"She went in the pool to learn how to swim."

"Oy that girl never listens. How do you know? You vere vit her, right?"

"I was going to teach her to swim when Aunt Sarah came along and pulled her out. It was very mean."

"You shouldn't have done dat."

"Mommy lets me swim. It's always okay if I go into the pool."

"So, go in ven the lifeguards can vatch you and don't take your little cousin vere she doesn't belong.

Every mother has her own rules and you gotta listen to dem."

"Grandma, you're the mother of both our mothers so aren't your rules the most important?"

"You don't vant to know from dat because I tink no children should go in public pools to catch polio. Dis time, vit you, your mother vins. Vat can I do?"

Rachel put one arm around her grandmother while using her other arm to reach over Grandma's shoulder to take a hot roll.

"No hugs, remember. And put back the roll or give it to your skinny cousin. I don't vant you should get fat."

Rachel returned the bread and twirled to leave.

"Vait," her grandmother said. "I have someting for you and Leah. I tink maybe tonight is the right time to give it to you. See me in our bungalow just before dinner. I vill tell Sarah so she vill let Leah come, too."

Sometimes, Grandma was the best, giving Rachel extra treats and letting her stay up late. Other times, she yelled at her to read a book and not be like her mother who quit school at age 14. Rachel hoped this would be one of her grandmother's kinder moments, like when she combed her hair after a bath because her mother was too busy getting *faputzed* (dolled up) for the evening. Or when she took them to the bakery area to get *rugelach*. Which one would it be tonight?

That evening the two cousins met outside the bungalow. Leah took her cousin's hand and together they walked, almost marched, inside. Instinctively, they kept their heads down, though they didn't know why. The swimming problem seemed to be over—for now. And since Grandma said she had a gift for them, this visit would be a good thing. The girls did not get many presents so they were extra curious. It wasn't a birthday or Chanukah. It wasn't any holiday. What could it be?

"I have for you someting special," Grandma said while tucking a stray strand of hair under her kerchief.

There was nothing in her hand so the girls were a bit confused.

"I vant you to vear it all the time. May it protect you."

It sounded like she was saying a prayer or a song. Leah wondered if the present was just words and she would have to pretend she liked them.

"And don't forget, your grandmother bought for you such a present," she said as she touched the gold chain around her neck, the one she wore every day.

"Grandpa gave me this necklace before vee vere married, before vee vere engaged," Grandma said while making sure the cousins could get a good look at it. "He said I was his *shayna maidel,* his pretty girl, and he wanted me to have something to know he vas vit me, tinking about me all the time."

Leah and Rachel lifted their heads and looked at each other. Then they watched Grandma put her hands inside the pockets of her patterned housedress and pull out two small identical boxes.

"See, Grandma. It's good to have pockets," Leah said.

"I see," Grandma said. "This is not for your birtday. It is only because you are such gut girls. Real gold. 24-carets. Just like mine."

She handed a box to each child.

"Vit dis present you should know I'm alvays vit you, like Grandpa is vit me. Dis is to remind you who you are and vere you come from. Remember, vee are from the same family and family rules are more important den any other rules. Do you understand? Ven you vill touch your necklace like I do, you vill know that family is everyting."

The girls looked at each other again and giggled. Together they bobbed their heads up and down while counting—one, two, three—then tore off the white bows and opened their gifts at exactly the same time.

Inside each velvet-lined box was a thin gold chain with a tiny Star of David.

7. Secrets Always Come Out

Momism: Relationships are complicated.

"I don't understand why you won't come with me," Kevin said while making two cups of coffee on our Keurig that was nestled in a corner of the Alaska-white granite counter top.

"Not interested," I said taking one cup.

"You always like attending black-tie benefits. Gives us a chance to practice our dance moves after all the lessons we've had," he said with a smile and a twist of his hips, then gave me a nudge with his shoulder, gentle enough not to spill my coffee. It felt playful and made me appreciate his consistent affection. At the same time, I remembered my near blunder in Italy with Roberto and a wave of guilt washed over me.

It seemed surreal that I had taken a waiter to my hotel room, saw him naked, got into bed together. Thank goodness I kicked him out before we went any further. What I did wasn't cheating. Almost, but not really. That episode is finished and I must stop agonizing over it.

"Honey, you're off in your own thoughts again," Kevin said as he sat down on one of our high, charcoal-gray leather and chrome stools. Max plopped himself at my husband's feet, creating a peaceful scene perfect enough for a design magazine.

I shook my head, too wrapped up in my anxiety to accept Kevin's attempt to be nice, wishing I could snap out of whatever was spoiling everything.

"When you wanted a few days by yourself in Florence, I did as you wished because I love you," Kevin said. "Waiting to join you later was really hard."

"I know. My going alone was so out of character."

"It made me wonder if there are secrets you might have," he said, pursing his lips, avoiding my eyes.

I wanted to hug him, reassure him there is nothing undisclosed between us, though to do so would have been a big fat lie. Hiding the transgression in Italy made me think of my younger sister who was buried so long ago and that my husband and children knew nothing about.

"You're my rock. Always have been and always will be," I said, hoping I didn't sound phony.

I hated the tension between us and was mad at myself for turning Kevin's simple request into what I call a discussion with emphasis. I was making my decision about attending an event bigger than it needed to be.

We bickered back and forth, then escalated, exchanging philosophical ideas about life and marriage, men versus women—one of those useless conversations that lead nowhere because each participant has already taken a side. We debated until Kevin shrugged and tried the old smiling trick, pretending everything was okay when everything was really on hold. Then I decided to do the right thing, to be better for him.

"I'll go to the black-tie event with you," I said. "I might wear red, a noisy color that exudes confidence, even if I don't feel it."

"Any color will do as long as you put on one of your fancy gowns and join me."

I was glad he softened his voice.

"It'll be fun to go together, hold hands again, be a happy couple," he said, then shifted topics. "But what were you thinking?"

"You mean in Florence or just now?" I said, making sure we were talking about the same thing.

"Florence was months ago," he said, looking bewildered. "I'm asking you what you were thinking just now."

"Not much."

"I'm not so sure," he said. "Now that you have a new project, it's time for you to buck up."

"My store is not a project. It's my next career."

"Call it whatever you want."

The mood was no longer comfortable. Kevin had aired his fears about my private time in Italy and I had skirted revealing anything. Then I thought about the formal fundraiser I had just agreed to go to and my negative demons returned.

"I'll go to the dance, but try to put yourself inside my head, watching everyone admire *you* while I have no professional identity."

"Oh boy," Kevin said, placing his empty cup in the sink, leaving it for me to move into the dishwasher. "Here we go again."

"Oh boy is right. I'm angry that I lost my job. At the same time, I feel guilty for not supporting you. I want to be kinder. All I am is a mess," I said in a whisper, setting my elbows on the counter and resting my chin on my hands.

"Honey, you're not a mess," he said, placing his arm around me. "You just need to readjust your definition of success. With this store, you'll have a whole new experience. You're moving forward, one dress at a time. Come to the benefit and talk about your boutique. You'll create customers."

I knew he was right, though I still felt lost. Here I was, in the middle of my life, believing my best days were behind me. On the outside, it looked like I had it all. On the inside, there was so much sadness, a void I didn't know how to fill. I couldn't stop continuing on automatic pilot in the wrong direction.

"I'll still be in your shadow until *Susanna's* is a success," I said, raising my voice above the sound of sirens that screamed up from Park Avenue into our apartment through the closed windows.

"Enough!" Kevin shouted.

His anger and frustration jolted me. It was time to stop whining.

"You're right," I said. "I can talk about the store and Francesca's designs. I'll come with you and keep my head high."

We hugged, awkwardly at first, then our love pushed us into a real embrace.

I felt a little better as we walked together to the entrance hall to take our semi-private elevator to the lobby.

A spring breeze brought a bit of calm as we strolled, hand in hand, to meet Jennifer and check on the progress in the store. After our morning discussion, I forced myself to think exclusively about the boutique.

The place looked pretty good considering it was only a week since we were allowed to continue our renovations. The atmosphere already felt airy. Unfortunately, there was still much to do. Though the walls were plastered they needed paint. New molding was in place near the ceiling and the floor still had to be sanded and stained. High hats were in boxes to be installed in addition to modern chandeliers. Mirrors had not been delivered yet. That was okay since the dressing rooms still required finishing touches.

"Francesca suggested an orange couch," Kevin said.

"I know," I said, envisioning white couches like the ones in our apartment. "A bright color is not in my comfort zone."

"As your designer, perhaps Francesca is spot-on."

"Maybe. Maybe it's time to jump over my shadow and surprise her with the couch when she comes back for the opening party."

Thank goodness Roberto was not coming with her.

8. Summer, 1954

As Leah watched her Aunt Dina light the braided candle, she started to tap her foot, then her fingers against her thigh at the same time, anxious to get to dinner and then the show to hear her cousin Rachel sing.

"Vat is wrong vit you?" her grandmother asked. "You're jumping like a grasshopper. It's *Shabbos*. Stay still, *shayna* von."

When Leah saw her grandmother's bent fingers coming toward her cheek to give an affectionate pinch, Leah moved her head. She glared at her aunt, trying to send a mental message to hurry with the Havdalah ceremony separating the holy Shabbat from the ordinary rest of the week.

"It seems like your mother is moving in slow motion," Leah whispered to her cousin.

"That's the way she always does it," Rachel said. "Slowly. It's so annoying and takes forever. If Grandpa hurries with his prayers over the wine we can taste our grape juice."

Leah saw her father look at his watch. He was not as religious as her mother, and Leah knew he also wanted the ceremony to be over.

They watched Grandpa pour the wine, a *segulah* or good omen, then say the blessings in Hebrew before taking a sip.

"We saw the fire of the candle, we felt its heat, we heard the blessings and we tasted the wine," Rachel whispered in a rapid sing-song voice. "Almost done."

Grandpa put his finger over his mouth to remind them to be quiet.

"You sound like my friend, Esther, when she comes over on a Saturday night," Leah said, picking up the sweet spice box, enjoying the fragrance of the cloves before passing the silver container to Rachel.

"Okay, we smelled it. That's the fifth sense. We're finished," Rachel said as she wished everyone a *Gute Vokh*.

"Have a good week," Leah said, refusing to use the Yiddish words that were mixed with English whenever she was with her grandparents. She understood what they said. It's how she grew up, but the foreign language upset her. She wanted to be an American, not an immigrant. She was born here. Her parents were born here so she didn't understand why she had to adopt her grandparents' ways. She knew her father, Solly, agreed. He made her feel better when he smiled while patting her on top of her shiny brown hair.

Aunt Dina frowned at Leah then turned toward Rachel.

"Hurry to the PA system and make your announcement," she said.

Rachel grabbed Leah's hand and ran with her to the office where she turned on the hotel loud speaker.

"Dinner is now being served in the main dining room," Rachel said in her most grown-up voice. She paused to count to ten very slowly, as she had been instructed, then repeated the message.

"Dinner is now being served in the main dining room."

It was an easier message than the midweek ones like, *anyone who wants to play volleyball please go to the volleyball court* or *Bingo will begin in the card room immediately following afternoon coffee and cake.*

Before Rachel had a chance to turn off the speaker, Leah grabbed the microphone and imitated her cousin, "There will be no dinner in the main dining room." Her giggles boomed in every part of the hotel. "Only kidding," she added.

"Now you've got me in trouble," Rachel said. "We didn't have permission for you to say anything. You can't make a joke about dinner. My mother will be so mad."

"I bet my mother will laugh," Leah said. "It was such fun. I want to do it again."

"No!" Rachel said, grabbing the microphone.

Leah pulled the microphone out of Rachel's hand and said, "There's only food for fifty, so hurry up."

Rachel looked like she was about to cry.

"Only kidding," Leah announced before Rachel turned off the loud speaker, ready to yell at her cousin. Leah quickly changed the subject.

"How do you remember the words to the songs when you're on stage? I don't think I could. The memory part, I mean. It must be harder than singing and harder than knowing how to act."

"It's easy for me and everyone says I have a good voice. I'm not bragging. It's what they say."

"It's your parents' hotel so maybe that's why they say you're so good."

"That's mean. I know I get to sing because I'm the daughter of the owner."

"Doesn't that bother you?" Leah said.

"No. I don't care as long as I get to be on stage. I love it. And I'm loud, too. You can hear me without a microphone," Rachel said.

Rachel bent her head down toward her cousin so they could talk while they rushed to the dining room. It was supposed to be special to eat with the grownups, a treat that happened only because it was the family cousin's club meeting.

"I don't care about eating. I just want to go to the show," Leah said. "I didn't hear you sing the last time we visited."

"That was a year ago. You were only six and not allowed to stay up so late."

"Well, tonight, I'm going to stay awake even if I have to sneak out when nobody's looking."

"I could never do that," Rachel said. "If my mother caught me, she would send me to my room for a long time."

"Going to your room is no big deal. I always get sent there."

"Why?"

"Because I never listen, that's why."

By now the girls had reached the dining room. They had to stop before entering because Rachel was out of breath from running and started to cough. Once inside, they were disappointed because most of the tables were full and the girls couldn't find a place where they could sit together.

"Can we eat in the kitchen?" Rachel asked her mother. "The waiters and busboys take care of us and I can show Leah secret places in the walk-in pantry."

"Absolutely not," Dina said, sounding abrupt just like Grandma only without an accent. "This is a special weekend with all our cousins. You will eat with us. Leah will sit with her parents and you will sit at our table. We've saved seats for each of you. Papa will join us while Mama stays in the kitchen to supervise the waiters."

Dinner was torture. The cousins wished the hotel kitchen would stick to their grandparents' Eastern European tradition of a quick, light meal on Saturday night. Since most of the guests were of German Jewish heritage, they celebrated the new week in a more modern way. Besides, this was a festive hotel environment. Dinner was always a big deal, a way for the guests to get their money's worth. It would not be quick.

Leah watched her father consume both vegetable soup and chopped liver with the best rolls ever. She loved bread so much she ate three pieces. When she looked over at Rachel's table, she saw Aunt Dina take bread out of Rachel's hand. Dina was always stopping Rachel from eating something. Her cousin wasn't skinny, but she also wasn't fat. It couldn't be so bad to have one more roll or cookie.

"Mommy, can I have another roll?" Leah said.

"Yes, darling. Of course, you can," her mother said while flicking her blonde hair out of her eyes. "If you promise to save room for the steak."

Leah nodded, then put the extra bread into her pocket to give to her cousin. She just had to make sure Aunt Dina didn't catch her.

The waiters came out with meat and side dishes. There were so many options each table needed two waiters. They served carrots with honey, spinach with garlic and *kishke* made with vegetables, chicken fat, spices and onion encased like a sausage. There also were potatoes with parsley, herbed mushrooms with white wine, brussels sprouts and applesauce. The parade of food seemed endless.

At last, the guests sauntered down to the bar area. Tables and chairs were arranged around the room, cabaret style. The dance team and comedians were behind the curtain on either side of the stage. The Social Director, always a big help to Rachel, was testing the microphone. After she welcomed everyone, she introduced Rachel who walked on stage in her favorite blue dress. A giant blue bow was clipped to the top of her blonde ponytail.

Rachel appeared calm when her relatives clapped and cheered. She simply curtseyed and thanked them, then lifted the microphone off the stand and held it close to her mouth. Most important, the five-piece band was in front of the stage where Rachel could see the bandleader. He had taught her the songs and directed her presentation. She was not allowed to begin until he nodded.

This evening was different because so many of the guests were family. Rachel didn't have to sing songs in German for the German refugees, some with numbers tattooed on their arms. She didn't have to sing a Viennese song. Instead, she had prepared two Yiddish numbers and two popular English pieces. Eddie Fisher had made one of her selected songs famous, so everyone would know the words and maybe sing with her.

The cousins who came to the hotel every summer came with an abundance of musical talent. Leah's father played the saxophone. Others played mandolin, accordion, piano, violin and clarinet. Even tambourines counted as an instrument in this crowd. Music was their major form of entertainment. And none of them ever had lessons.

The minute Rachel started to sing, *Belz, Mayn Shtelele Belz* (My Little Town of Belz), an uncle stood from his chair in the audience and played the clarinet, taking some attention away from Rachel. Next someone else stood and played the accordion. Leah's father played his saxophone, while another uncle joined with his violin. All four extra musicians were standing, delivering notes simultaneously from their spots in the audience.

At first Rachel kept singing. The relatives' impromptu band was loud, drowning out her voice. Leah saw her cousin start to cry and heard her cough. The music stopped and the room was quiet, no shuffling of feet or seats creaking even though people adjusted their positions. The silence was awkward.

"You're a big girl," Leah mouthed from her center seat in the front row, not sure if Rachel could see her with the lights out over the audience. "You can be better than all these silly uncles," she added.

Rachel nodded at her cousin, then stood taller, appearing to push away her feelings and gain control.

"Excuse me," she said into the microphone, and started to sing again. The hotel band quickly joined her while the uncles sat quietly.

At the end of the show, after Dina gave Rachel a big hug, Leah heard Grandma tell her cousin she was brave on stage, a real spitfire, which was a modern fancy word for fiery temper that her grandparents had picked up and used to mean strong-willed.

She remembered Grandma was the first to get out on a dance floor or play her tambourine or spoons with her relatives when they played *klezmer* music. That's when Grandpa first called her a spitfire. And Leah knew their neighbor called his daughter, Esther, a spitfire because she liked to do everything her own way. He said she had a mind of her own.

That American-sounding word was good for her aunt, too. Sometimes Dina and Grandma yelled at each other. A lot. Dina liked to smoke, except cigarettes upset Grandma who shouted "*feh*" so loud everyone nearby could hear. Her aunt did whatever she wanted to do anyway.

Another time Dina cut her own hair in a new style called a bob. Leah liked how her aunt looked even though it made her grandmother mad. When Grandma saw Dina's modern hairdo, the waiters and busboys could hear them scream at each other from the kitchen. Leah and Rachel heard the shouts all the way out on the lawn.

When her aunt bought the latest shoes with buckles on them, Grandma yelled again. Aunt Dina always fought back, shouting that Mama didn't understand and something about the next generation.

Just like Dina, Leah planned to smoke real cigarettes when she grew up. Her daddy promised to teach her how. She also hoped to have nice clothes instead of things her mother sewed. Leah thought that only a girl with a mind of her own would make jokes on the loud speaker. She was glad she had done it and if she ever had a problem when she got older, she hoped to be as brave as cousin Rachel was on stage tonight. Maybe they were both spitfires.

9. Grown-ups Grow Away

Momism: Family is everything.

"Mom," Jennifer said, as we left the boutique. "Let Dad walk ahead. I have something important to discuss."

"You know, whatever it is, you can tell both of us. We're a team."

Jennifer slowed down and gulped fresh air in a nervous way.

"I already told Dad," she said. "Now I want to tell you."

I was a bit annoyed that Kevin knew something ahead of me again, but this wasn't the time to point out the obvious. Instead, I waited. Not an easy thing for me to do.

"Are you pregnant? Will Dad and I be grandparents?" I said. "You can count on me to babysit at least one day a week, perhaps two after the store is doing well enough for me to hire a manager. Is it a boy or a girl?"

"Mom, stop. I've been married four months. I don't want a child yet."

"A child? You must have more than one. You must. And why not now?"

"I want to hold off until my career is more established."

"Oh honey, a job can end abruptly. Don't make the mistake of substituting a career for kids. Don't become one of those women who carry around a little dog as if it were a baby."

"No little dog and I'm not substituting anything. I just want to wait."

"You're already 30."

"Exactly. I knew you'd understand."

"Understand what?"

"Understand why I'm going to freeze my eggs."

"What did you just say?"

When we reached the corner of Park and 79th we stopped. Jennifer turned to face me, ignoring the walk sign.

"I said I'm going to freeze my eggs."

I stayed silent, trying to keep all expression from my face, waiting for her to continue, not wanting to escalate to a shouting match amidst other people passing by. This was not how I had lived my life and not how I expected my daughter to live hers.

"Many of my friends are doing it," she said, as if that gave the process legitimacy.

"Your friends? Maybe women over 40 or those needing treatment for cancer. Maybe single women not in a relationship or needing to have their heads examined," I said, hearing my voice get louder and feeling that anxiety-driven red rash form on my face. "Not you. Not my married daughter. I won't hear of this."

"Well, Mom, it's not up to you. Besides, I read that the healthiest babies are conceived when the mother is between 24 and 32 years old. Freezing is only just-in-case."

"Just in case what? And doesn't it cost a fortune?"

"Probably over $10,000. Daddy said he'd pay for it."

"Not if I can help it," I said, clenching my teeth like my mother used to do and stamping my foot. I would have screamed at Kevin, but he was too far ahead of us.

"Dad said you'd try to stop me. That's exactly why I didn't tell you," Jennifer said in almost a shriek. "You're always trying to control me, change what I do. I was going to inform you a week ago. Then Francesca arrived and everyone was so busy with the store, the skeleton and the police."

"You told Daddy, and not me. You knew about Sean's girlfriend and I didn't. What's happening here? Why is my family leaving me out?"

She's entitled to have secrets, Mom said, *much like we do*.

"Oh Mom, Mom, Mom," Jennifer said, "you're not left out. I'm telling you now. You have your own ideas about how Sean and I should live. Sometimes it's easier to fill you in after the fact. You know that old saying, do it now and beg forgiveness later."

"After the fact! Beg forgiveness later! Did you freeze your eggs already?"

"No. I have an appointment with a doctor next week."

"I'm going with you."

"No, you're not. Don't worry. It's very common. Some women even have egg freezing parties."

"You've got to be kidding."

"It's no joke."

"What do they do at these parties?"

"The guests compare research about reproductive endocrinologists and share information on what to expect."

"Have you gone to one of these so-called parties?"

"No. Not my style. I'm more like you, do my own research."

"What did you find?"

"I don't want to bother you with details. Just know it's pretty safe."

"PRETTY safe? You think I can't handle facts?"

"Okay. Here's an abbreviated version. The doctor figures out the best dosage of meds. Then I'll need to give myself shots and get monitored at the doctor's office for a few weeks before she retrieves my eggs."

"Oh, for God's sake, Jen. This is ridiculous. You have a husband."

Jennifer looked more crushed than angry. With much effort, I closed my mouth while I stepped aside to allow a dog walker with a dozen different breeds and sizes on a dozen leashes to pass us. In that brief moment I was able to calm down, hoping not to make an agonizing rift with my daughter. We'd been so close until she got married. Then the daily phone calls stopped. No questions about work or fashion. I no longer know what she does on weekends. Maybe the new distance is normal, but I feel as if I'm losing her.

"Mom, you don't get it."

"Obviously."

Jennifer stood there, pursing her lips and staring at her feet. I felt compelled to fill the silence.

"You have time to build a career and still become pregnant the natural way. Or do you plan to wait until you're 65 to conceive? You need a baby now, especially since I assume you'll have more than one."

"You're not being rational," she said, as a yellow taxi pulled up. My daughter looked at the cab then dismissed me with a flip of her wrist, or was it the taxi she was sending off?

"Mom, there's something else I have to tell you."

She turned to face me and our eyes locked. This was not a good sign.

"Adam and I are thinking of moving. To Seattle," she said, standing taller, as if she were ready for a fight. "I'm going to freeze my eggs with my doctors before we leave."

"Honey, your family is here. You love New York. You both have terrific jobs. Why move? Why choose a place with so much rain?"

"Adam got recruited by a top tech company and I can do marketing and public relations anywhere. I've already sent out my resume to a dozen companies," she said, twisting her hair and moving her weight from one foot to the other like she did when she was a little girl caught doing something off limits. If I weren't so upset, I'd have enjoyed the sweet memories.

"I'm going to lose you," I said, feeling my shoulders slump as I lowered my eyes. "I won't be part of my grandchildren's lives."

"Mom, you're not going to lose me. You'll come visit. We plan to have an extra bedroom for you and Dad. It's not about you. It's about Adam and me. Why can't you be happy for us?"

How could I show happiness when all I felt was dismay? This was not supposed to be the way things happened. I always imagined my children would live nearby, or maybe, if I lost influence, in the suburbs. I never allowed myself to picture my daughter on the west coast.

We stood in the middle of the sidewalk without speaking.

"Oh, I almost forgot," Jennifer said, handing me a slip of paper. "Here's the name and phone number of Sophie's dad."

"Who's Sophie?"

"Sean's girlfriend. Did you forget? Her father is a detective. I called and asked her for his number. Sean doesn't know, so don't tell him."

"I'm sick of secrets in this family. That's not how we brought you up," I said, while my own dark secret and the newer one in Italy flashed across my mind, yet again.

Don't tell, my mom said. *Some secrets must never be shared.*

I placed the paper inside my handbag then watched Jennifer continue to shake her head while she walked toward Lexington Avenue to take the subway to work.

"Damn these high heels and my vanity," I said to myself as I tried to race ahead to catch up with Kevin, who blew me an air kiss before jumping into a cab to go to his office. He must have figured how aggravated I was at Jennifer's news and slipped away as fast as possible.

I stood on the street thinking about Sean, my second child, my baby who looks like me. I remembered when he became taller, less like a little boy, more like a protector. He'd go out with his friends, yet still talked through life's options with me, even if he chose not to take my advice. That slowed down when he went to medical school and then stopped, maybe because he now confides in Sophie. I had to convince Sean to introduce us, but my head was full with so many other things to do.

Clothes were scheduled to arrive from Italy tomorrow, way earlier than expected. I needed to warehouse the imported garments while we sorted them by style and size. Steaming and attaching price tags would have to wait until they were hung in the store.

As I walked over to Panera on East 86th Street to grab a cup of coffee, I decided to stop interfering with Jennifer's plans before I severed our special bond. This freezing eggs business was practically a done deal. Jennifer's husband was in agreement. Kevin was paying. My only choice was to be supportive or risk becoming a mother who loses her relationship with her child. That would be unbearable. I vowed to do better, to be a kinder self, not the out-of-control shrew I was turning into.

My thoughts shifted to the small skeleton. Maybe a mother lost her child in a horrific way. Some of its relatives must be alive, wondering what happened. At least my daughter was only moving to another state.

It wasn't like me to be sidetracked from my business goals, yet I felt myself drawn away from my problems into those of the unknown skeleton. Maybe smashing the wall was symbolic—breaking down a barrier from my old days so I could step into the next phase of my life.

Susan, that's ridiculous. All you did was orchestrate the merger of two stores into one, my mother said. *You have a lot to do. For God's sake, stay focused.*

I pushed her voice aside, clinging to the idea that because the skeleton was so distant from my own difficulties, it would be a good problem to tackle. Maybe it *was* time to hire the detective.

10. Summer, 1954

Leah didn't tell anyone that, the next day, she intended to sit alone on the train, a few seats in front of her grandparents who would speak to each other in Yiddish. So embarrassing. So unfair that her mommy and daddy would drive home without her just because she threw up on long car rides.

She would change her seat once they got settled. If Grandma didn't yank her by her arm to be closer to them, she was sure there would be no yelling and no fuss. She thought she could get away with it as long as they could see her. Meanwhile, she wanted to enjoy her last day in the country.

Learning to swim had been a disaster despite bringing her pink-dotted bathing suit. Too many people were around keeping an eye on her. Wherever she went, there was a cousin or aunt or uncle watching, watching, watching.

Before she had gone to the country, her downstairs neighbor, Esther, had bragged that she knew how to swim. And she was younger. Sometimes Leah was jealous of Esther because she had four brothers and a sister so her parents couldn't watch all of them all the time.

Leah thought it wasn't fair to be an only child and have to make believe her cousin was her sister. She hoped she and Rachel could come up with a plan to escape all those eyes on their last day. It would be such fun to pretend to be old enough to be on their own.

"Let's hang out in the kitchen," Rachel said. "The busboys are so nice. They'll talk to us. And my mother won't see every cookie I put into my mouth."

"We can pretend we're glamorous with lots of boyfriends," Leah said.

"One day, we will be. Right now, we're still girls eating chocolate *babka* away from our parents. That's just as much fun."

"How do you know?"

"Know what?"

"Know that eating something sweet is as good as being glamorous, dressed in wonderful new clothes."

"Well, I don't really know. I think I know," Rachel said as she munched on a piece of cake, then started to cough.

"You're always coughing," Leah said. "You're supposed to cover your mouth when you cough."

"I'm not always coughing. The crumbs got stuck. They went down the wrong way."

"What way is the wrong way?"

"I don't know."

"You have one throat. Whatever you eat goes down, not sideways. Just one way—down."

"It felt weird."

"You're weird."

"Am not,"

"Are too," Leah said. "Let's play hide and seek. Close your eyes and count to ten. Then try to find me."

"Okay, but I know all the hiding places here better than you do. I'm going to find you so fast, I'll win this silly game."

Leah decided not to hide in the pantry. Instead, she tiptoed toward the bakery. The smell was so wonderful she didn't care if she got caught. Well, almost didn't care. Inside she saw movable racks of metal shelves. One was empty. Not a good place to hide. Another was filled with thick *challahs*. Perfect. She hoped they were still warm. After Rachel found her, maybe they could share an entire braided bread. She decided to eat some while she waited.

When she knelt down to tear off a piece of challah resting on the bottom shelf, she saw someone had dropped a white cloth or apron. She covered herself with whatever it was and kept quiet. Of course, that was the moment her nose decided to itch. It never bothered her when she didn't hide. Now it felt like someone had a feather and was tickling her. She was afraid to scratch because if Rachel were nearby, she would see the movement. This wasn't as much fun as she had imagined.

While Leah was quiet, she heard two people talking near the *rugelach* section. One sounded like her Aunt Dina. She wasn't sure who the other person was, probably one of their many cousins.

"It could be a real problem," Aunt Dina said. "Three people, from three different families, had to leave because they got sick. They'll tell their friends and nobody will come here."

"Just because they left with coughs doesn't mean they have tuberculosis. There are lots of reasons why people cough."

"If it does turn out to be TB, we'll be in trouble. Big trouble. I don't want our guests to get sick. It's my responsibility to keep everyone healthy. I'm sending

Mama and Papa home tomorrow. All I need is for Mama to start yelling at some inspector, screaming in Yiddish and broken English while pointing her finger. She's so frightened of authority she's liable to try to stop them from entering the hotel."

Leah didn't like what she heard. It scared her and she wanted to stand up and ask her aunt questions. At the same time, she was afraid to be seen where she didn't belong. She couldn't decide which was worse, listening or getting caught. Then the conversation continued.

"Are you forgetting she lived through a pogrom in Belarus? The Cossacks came on horseback and shot the Jews. Some brought dogs to help them find anyone who hid. Do you think that's why she tells the girls to stay away from dogs?"

"Of course," Dina said. "I'll never forget Mama's horrific stories. You can't imagine how many times she told me her older sister was found by a barking beast then beaten. By a soldier. When I think I know every detail of the family's flight across the country and across the ocean, she says there's more, then refuses to talk about it."

"How can you expect her not to be scared? Not to be afraid of authority?"

"Because part two of her story is how they succeeded in the garment industry and made enough money to provide us with a good life. They were the first in the family, and in the neighborhood, to own a car. She and Grandpa moved forward, yet she can't let go of her past even though it is less than a third of her life a long time ago."

The information Leah just heard about Grandma's sister was new. She didn't want to know any more so she covered her ears. It didn't help. She could still hear her aunt talking.

"I understand, but I was born HERE, in 1915. My life is not her life. Sometimes I feel like my mother's personal history is a burden that will never go away. I don't want to be like her even though I worry about her all the time."

"I thought you were worried about polio."

"That too," Dina said, taking out a cigarette from her case. "I'm very concerned about polio. The whole country is. As a precaution, I'm thinking about closing the pool for the last three weeks of the season, though that might cause our guests to panic."

"All the papers are reporting on the success of Salk's vaccine."

"I know. I'm sure lots more people will get the shot next year, including Rachel. That doesn't help us right now."

While they were talking, Leah started to crawl toward the door. Then she heard footsteps. She knew it must be her cousin and wanted to warn her not to come into the bakery. It was too late.

"Rachel," Dina said. "What are you doing here? Are you trying to get more *challah* or *rugelach*? You'll get very fat if you keep sneaking treats."

"Mommy, I'm looking for Leah. We're playing hide and seek."

"Go look somewhere else, *Bubala*. She's not here. Are you sure you aren't trying to get something extra to eat?"

Rachel nodded before scampering out. Leah waited a few minutes, then tore off a bigger piece of bread and, still covered with the cloth, continued to crawl toward the door. Dina saw the white apron moving across the cement floor.

"Leah, Aunt Dina yelled. "Where are you going with that bread? When a loaf is missing, we think a waiter or busboy took it. You don't want to get them in trouble, do you?"

Dina looked at what was left.

"You might as well keep it. You're so skinny I'll be happy if you eat the whole thing. Now go. Go find Rachel and think of somewhere else to play."

Leah was surprised she didn't get sent to her room. It seemed like her aunt was nicer to her niece than to her own daughter. She threw off the apron and stood up. On her way out she bumped smack into Rachel who was standing in the doorway.

"It's not fair," Rachel said. "You get all the extra food and I get yelled at. When you go home tomorrow, it's going to be a hard three weeks. Nobody will sneak treats for me. At least I can go swimming."

"I'm not going home tomorrow."

"You're not? That's great. How did you get to stay?"

"Only kidding. I'm really sad I have to leave. And you're not going swimming. Your mother is closing the pool."

"Is that another joke? It's not nice to trick me all the time."

"It's real. I heard her talking to someone, maybe one of the cousins," Leah said.

"I guess she's afraid people will get sick if they swallow the water."

"Who swallows pool water?"

"Everyone. Not on purpose. Sometimes it happens. You'll see when you learn how to swim," Rachel said.

"You better swim today, before your mother empties it tomorrow."

"Why tomorrow? The hotel is open for three more weeks."

"Someone from the government is coming to inspect the hotel. Besides, you don't want to catch something. Just dip your toes."

The girls ran over to the pool to dunk their feet. Rachel ran faster and left Leah behind. When Leah caught up, her cousin was sitting on the cement edge. She was out of breath and coughing.

"You don't sound so good," Leah said. "Maybe you should come home with us."

"I don't want to go home. Home reminds me school starts soon. Then I have to get a polio shot. You, too, right?"

Just then, Grandma appeared carrying a jar of Gulden's mustard, a spoon and two cotton towels. Her red print dress billowed in the breeze that made her apron flap.

"*Bubala,* I heard you coughing again," she said to Rachel. "I vant you should put on your chest this mustard plaster. Already I added an egg and vater and made von towel vet."

Rachel lay back in an area shaded by a large maple tree. She let her grandma put the wet towel on her so the plaster wouldn't burn her skin. She made a funny face when she felt the mustard mixture being spread and covered with the second towel, then thanked her grandma for taking such good care of her. Once Grandma left, the girls started giggling.

"Do I smell?" Rachel asked.

"Not as bad as when Grandma stuck my sprained ankle into a bowl of vinegar. I had to sit and sit and sit, soaking my whole foot for over an hour. How can you thank her and be so nice to her?"

"Because of Grandma, I don't have to go to a doctor every time something little happens. Why are you always making faces behind her back?"

Leah ignored the question. "Your cough doesn't sound little," she said.

"How do you know? Just because you're turning eight doesn't mean you're an expert about coughs."

"Am too."

"Are not," Rachel said, while leaning on one arm and keeping the top towel on her chest with the other.

"By the time I see you in New York, I'll be all better. Maybe you'll go to synagogue with me. I don't know why I have to go while my mother and grandmother can stay home."

"They need to cook," Leah said.

"Last time the police came because bad people painted nasty words on the side of the building."

"It's scary to go alone," Leah said.

"I know. Thank goodness I'm only alone on the walk there. Wanna know a secret?"

"Sure. Do I have to keep it to myself?"

"That's what a secret is," Rachel said.

"What is it?"

"You mean my secret?"

"Yes. What else would I mean?" Leah said.

"I like sitting upstairs with the women," Rachel said. "I don't have to pay attention and I don't have to listen to anyone."

"That's your secret? God knows you're not listening. Aren't you supposed to like the prayers?"

"Not me. For me, the best part is having lunch with everyone after the service. Then I get to walk home from *shul* with Grandpa, which is fun—unless he asks me what I learned."

Leah nodded. "I have a secret, too."

"You do! What is it? Tell me!"

"Okay, but you have to keep it to yourself. You can't tell anyone."

"I know. I told YOU what a secret is."

Leah waited, fiddled with her hair then got close to Rachel to whisper. "I like a waiter."

"No! Which one?"

"The one who served my table last night in the main dining room."

"That's Jacob. He's nice. And friendly."

"He served me an extra dessert," Leah said. "You have to help me figure out how to eat in the main dining room again. It's my last night here."

The girls saw Grandma returning to check on the mustard plaster so Rachel lay back with her arms at her sides while Leah moved into the sun to dangle her feet, pretending to be swimming in the pool that would soon be closed.

11. So Many Differences

Momism: Perfect is different for everyone.

"Thank you for seeing me, John," I said, while picking at a half Fuji apple chicken salad with the dressing on the side.

I hoped I didn't appear as nervous as I felt sneaking behind my son's back, asking his girlfriend's father to lunch. Do it now, beg forgiveness later. That's what Jennifer suggested and here I was, following her poor advice. I'll tell Sean tomorrow.

Meanwhile, I was glad John and I were by ourselves. I chose to meet at *Panera* over on East 86th Street because it's casual, has coffee I like and most important, is cheap. I doubted the man would let me pick up the tab and I didn't want to impose a hefty bill on someone who lives on a detective's salary, whatever that is. I wondered how he could afford medical school for his daughter or if she were carrying substantial student loans.

"It's only been a few days since the skeleton was discovered. I'm rather unraveled by it," I said, pushing a stray strand of hair behind my ear. Ever since I opted for a chin-length cut in Italy, I had to fuss. "Sometimes the mystery is far from my thoughts. Other times I feel compelled to find out what happened. My husband doesn't understand why I care and the police won't tell me anything."

"Well ma'am, I'm happy to help, if I can," he said, speaking in a booming voice that would be great for commercials. Then he adjusted his clear-framed eyeglasses, stretched his long legs under the table and cracked his knuckles. I clenched my teeth.

"Do you mind not calling me ma'am?" I said. "It makes me feel old."

"No problem," he said, with a laugh. "As long as we're being open, I'm afraid I'm with your husband on this. Why get in the middle of somethin' that happened long ago and has nothin' to do with you."

I didn't have a good answer, yet I wanted to look smart. John was not just a retired detective. He might become a future in-law. While I was on a mission to get his help, I also wanted to learn about him and of course, make a good impression.

"You don't know me. I'm pretty grounded, not into crystals and fortune telling," I said, realizing I sounded odd. "But since the skeleton was discovered in my store, it feels like there's an unseen force compelling me to solve this mystery."

John's continuous eye contact made me keep talking without waiting to hear his response.

"At the moment, my life is upside down. I don't know if Sean told you, I no longer work at the ad agency. Did that for 25 goal-oriented years. Now, ready or not, it's time for a change."

If John knew I had not left my job on my own, he chose to keep quiet.

"Managing a store will be my next career, my new professional identity."

I wondered if this man ever thought about someone's professional identity or if he had any idea what I was talking about. Regardless, I couldn't stop pouring out my feelings. When he leaned back and smiled, I exhaled much of my anxiety.

"Funny you should say that. It's so far from what I believe."

"What do you mean?"

"I mean I'm me, with or without my job," he said with his enormous grin. "I was happy with my work, enjoyed living life with my wife and family. Now I'm retired and still enjoy life with my wife and family. Only difference is more time to go fishing."

I couldn't accept that he was content to leave a job he liked. Maybe I could learn something from this man.

"I think knowing what happened to the skeleton will prove significant," I said, shifting back to the reason for our meeting. "I believe finding out what happened will provide a vital clue to—oh—to I don't know what," I said, aware I was coming across as less than rational.

"Sounds heavy. Not into psychological stuff. I can try to help unravel the hidden facts. Just not sure I want to. Not interested in competing with my police friends or going back to work."

"We both have children," I said, trying to appeal to his parental side. "Judging from the size of the bones, the skeleton probably belongs to a kid. Some members of its family might be alive, maybe the mother or more likely, a sibling. I think they deserve closure. They're entitled to know what happened so they can mourn their loss and move on in a healthier way."

"Seems like you're inserting your own feelings upon this family, though we know nothing about them."

I nodded. "Could be."

"Also, finding facts will take time," he said.

"That's okay. I'll open as planned, with or without answers."

"Might become a distraction from your store."

"I won't let it. I'm no detective, which is why I called you to find out what happened. And of course, I'll pay you."

"No, no, no," he said, looking down at his large hands resting on the table. Then he stared at me, almost right through me, with his magnetic blue eyes. "Can't take your money. You're like family."

"Our kids are just dating, not engaged," I said, trying to soften my words with a weak smile, hoping I didn't sound rude. I sipped coffee from my size large paper cup to take time to steady my emotions before meeting his gaze. I wondered if his daughter had his eyes and hoped she didn't have his broad shoulders. I cursed the combination of my mother's superficial ideals and working in an ad agency that made me give so much importance to appearances.

"At least the kids don't know we'll be doing this together," I said.

"They know."

"What? What do you mean they know?"

"Told them last night, at dinner. They decided it was a great idea. The kids think we're so different we won't get along. They hope we'll find common ground if we take this on as a team."

"Of course we're different," I said, sounding angry, wishing I could keep my mouth shut.

I pushed away thoughts of a detective vs. a plastic surgeon; his wife, a nurse vs. me, an ex corporate executive. What I didn't know, I made up: our country club and golf vs. their bowling and who knows what else. Republican vs. Democrat, beer vs. scotch. None of these differences affected my friendships with other people. When it comes to blending families, that's another situation. I wondered what generic criticisms he attributed to us because we probably are more affluent. Bet he thinks we're stuffy and cold, even formal. Kevin always wears a blazer, so maybe we are.

"You say you had dinner with Sean last night. Was that the first time?" I said.

"Had him over three or four evenings. A lovely young man. Not as tall as we would have liked for our Sophie," he said, with a pause and a laugh, pushing back his dark gray hair that was peppered with streaks of white and long enough to cover his ears. "Real kind and real smart. You must be very proud of him."

"Yes," I said, hiding that I felt left out. This girl's parents already were acquainted with my son. All I knew so far is that his daughter is a student at medical school. Sean is six feet tall, like Kevin. I wondered how tall Sophie was.

You get what you give, I heard my mom say. *If you're critical, the next generation runs away. That's why we spared you disapproval.*

"Hello," John said, interrupting my daydreaming."

"Seems a bit unfair that you know Sean while I haven't met Sophie," I said, not daring to let on that I had looked her up online.

"I'm certain you'll meet soon. Maybe Sean's concerned you'll be tough on my daughter. He's making us worried about that, too. Now that we've met, I think it'll go smoothly."

I nodded, hoping he was right.

"Well, if you won't take cash, can we barter skills?" I said.

"Like what?"

"Like maybe Kevin can smooth out the scar on your cheek in exchange for your time as a detective."

"You're talking about this little line," he said with a wink while stroking his face with his finger. "It's a badge of honor for me. Stopped a psychopath from killing a young girl. A little gash is part of my profession. Besides, a perfectly smooth face leaves out all of life's stories."

"Oh," I said, touching my smooth forehead that was filled with Botox.

"Let's just consider my suggestion one of our many differences and move on," I said, feeling my face flush with that damn rash, wishing I could start this meeting over.

"No problem," he said with a half smile.

It felt as if he were amused by my tactless suggestion.

"If you work on this case for free, I'll owe you one," I said, looking down at my perfectly manicured hands, biting my bottom lip.

"You want to keep score, that's okay with me. I prefer to do the right thing and leave it at that. Bet you'll suffer, feeling indebted and working on something out of your control."

He delivered this insight with the most amazing full grin. I guess that's why I was able to tolerate what sounded like criticism even though it was the truth.

"After you called, a buddy I used to work with let me read the police report. The bigger problem is getting the team to let me participate going forward. I don't belong there anymore. Not sure I want to push into their territory."

"I hear you," I said, admiring his honorable values as well as his candor. "Can we at least consider what our next steps should be, in case you do decide to help?"

"Sean told me you were a corporate executive. Didn't tell me you're persistent. That's good when working on a case. Once we learn when the crime happened, we can do our own research. The skull and teeth will help determine illnesses as well as the age and race of the child. Fractures might indicate violence. The investigative officers probably checked for bullets or bullet casings. My pals at homicide or missing persons will let me know about fingerprints on the burgundy fabric."

"So, this means you'll do it. You'll help me."

"Still wavering."

I tried to keep my disappointment from showing.

"How long ago do you think the crime happened?"

"We don't know for sure it was a crime. Could be the child got stuck on its own. Sometimes the simplest answer is the right answer."

"This sounds like an Edgar Allen Poe story," I said, sorry I referred to an author in case he didn't like books.

"Prefer James Patterson novels. Let's not romanticize anything here," John said. "Maybe the person died before being placed in the wall. We might never find out why. A worse scenario is that it was still alive when it went inside."

"You have lots of theories," I said.

"'Cause we don't have enough facts. Must explore every possibility."

"Can I do something? My store is moving along at lightning speed thanks to a big tip I promised the workers, but there's still much to do. I can't open until the interior is complete. When I'm quiet, all I think about is my skeleton."

John paused for what felt like five minutes. I waited while he cracked his knuckles again and contemplated his options. Staying silent was not easy.

"Okay, as soon as I find out the approximate timeframe, you can check for newspaper articles about missing people in this neighborhood. You might have to go back as far as the 1950s or more. Someone would have written up this unsolved crime."

"That's a big research job," I said.

"Okay, here's an easier one for you. Find out who owned the building over the past fifty or so years. Who lived here? You're renting in one of the few brownstones left in the area. Bet there's a connection sitting right above the store."

"Why do you say that?"

"Experience and deductive reasoning. I don't believe in crystals or fortune tellers, either. I believe in intuition. Maybe we aren't as different as the kids think. Have to admit, I was braced to meet at a fancy restaurant."

Again, I asked, "Why do you say that?"

"Because you live on Park Avenue. Yet here we are, at one of my favorite places. Want to share a sweet?" he asked. "My wife, Nancy, and I indulge in chocolate cake as often as we can."

"No, thank you. I used up my mid-day calories on my salad," I said, wondering if his daughter also ate cake as often as she could.

12. Fall, 1954

"Mommy, I finished my homework. Can I go downstairs to play with Esther?" Leah said.

"Why not invite her up here?"

"She always comes here. I want to go to her apartment."

"Okay, but don't stay too long."

"How long is too long?"

Leah's mother laughed then hugged her. "Come back in an hour. That should be enough time. I want you home for supper."

"How will I know when it's an hour?"

"Leah, look at your new watch. When the big hand is on the 12 and the little hand is on the six, it will be six o'clock. That's when you must come upstairs to eat."

"Can't I eat with Esther?"

"Her mother has enough mouths to feed. Besides, I'm making noodles with butter, just like you like. And baby lamb chops with a nice big salad and your favorite soft rolls."

"Can I invite Esther to eat with us?"

"Not tonight, dear. They're kosher and we're not. She can't eat meat with dairy and I already buttered the noodles."

"Okay, Mommy. I won't stay too long," Leah said as she raced down the carpeted stairs. She was careful to hold on to the banister so she wouldn't fall, especially if she skipped a step or two.

When she knocked on Esther's door, she was unhappy that Esther's older sister, Malka, answered. Leah had secretly hoped Malka would not be home or at least would be helping her mother in their kitchen.

"Here comes trouble," Malka said, without a smile, as she let Leah in.

Malka was in high school and in charge of her brothers and sister when their mother was busy or out buying groceries. Malka was always angry and sometimes mean. For sure she was unpleasant to Leah, who didn't think of herself as trouble. Malka scared Leah.

"Come to my room," Esther said in a whisper, making her invitation sound special. "Malka has to cook dinner tonight, so she won't bother us."

The two girls hurried into the smallest bedroom that was in the front of the apartment, just like the room Leah's grandparents shared upstairs. Esther's parents had the big bedroom in back and their four sons shared the bedroom next to theirs.

Leah had never been inside the boys' room. She didn't care. She assumed it was just like hers only crowded with four kids instead of one. All she wanted from her neighbors was to play with Esther, watch their television, and stay away from Malka.

Once the girls stepped inside the bedroom, Esther shut the door.

"I don't want my brothers to come in," she said. "They like to tease me. Sometimes they make me cry."

"Well, I won't let them tease you when I'm here," Leah said, clenching her fists and moving them in the air like a boxer she once saw on TV. "I'll bop them on their heads and pretend I'm the school principal and send them to their room. Then I'll write a note to your mother."

"You will?" Esther said in awe.

"Only joking," Leah said, not sure she would know what to do to stop them from annoying their sister.

The two friends decided to play a board game. Esther took down Monopoly from a shelf near Malka's bed and opened it on the floor.

"I'm just learning how to play," Esther said. "You can help me if I mess up."

"I've only played two times with my cousin, Rachel. If we don't know what to do, we can make up our own rules."

"That wouldn't be Monopoly."

"So, we'll call it Ouropoly. It'll still be fun."

It took them awhile to divide up the money and select their pieces. Leah chose the thimble because her mother and grandmother both sewed. Esther kept switching between the iron and the Scottie dog, then settled on the dog because she wanted a real puppy, one she could walk and have as a best friend instead of just her stuffed dog.

For about 15 minutes, everything was quiet except for the sound of the dice rolling and whispered discussions about what properties to buy. When they got confused, they happily made up their own rules. Suddenly, Malka burst into the room. When she saw Esther and Leah playing Monopoly, she scrunched up her face and started to yell.

"That's MY game! How dare you take it from my shelf without asking me! You can't play with my things unless I give you permission."

Malka bent down, snatched the metal pieces and the cards and snapped the board shut. Then she organized the paper money to put the game away.

"Mama's out," she shouted. "I have to cook for everyone and I still have homework. Then I have to help the boys with their Hebrew lessons. It's not fair that you get to play just because you're only six and I'm 15. It's not fair I always do everything."

If Malka weren't so unpleasant, Leah would have felt sorry for her, maybe even volunteered to set the table, but Malka was almost always nasty.

Leah remembered the last time Esther visited upstairs. Cousin Rachel was there, too. They were having such a good time playing hide and seek until Malka banged on the door. Leah understood when a friend had to go home. But it was the loud, bossy way Malka gripped her little sister and dragged her away that upset Leah. Rachel agreed it was shameful. The cousins wondered if Malka was born like that.

One day Leah would be all grown up and move away and never have to see Malka again. Ever. This evening, Leah wanted to get out of that apartment. She grabbed Esther's hand and together the little girls scampered up the stairs to Leah's home where they sat down at the table next to Grandma and Grandpa.

Leah watched her mother purse her lips while setting another place. Once again, Leah had figured out how to get her way. She knew her mother was annoyed, but would not embarrass her in front of her friend. This would be discussed later, perhaps with another lecture about her being too strong-minded, whatever that meant.

Just then there was a knock at the door. Leah figured it would be someone from Esther's family so she wasn't surprised when she saw Malka.

"Esther," Malka said in too loud a voice, brushing past Sarah and standing near her sister. "You have to come home for dinner. I cooked a beef and vegetable stew. You have to eat with us. You have to stay kosher even when you're out of the house."

"But I want to eat here," Esther said, looking at a platter of steaming noodles in the center of the table.

"Sorry," Malka said, more in control of her emotions. "*Abba* is home and we're all together, except for you."

"I want to eat with Leah," Esther said softly.

"You always want to do whatever Leah does."

Malka gripped her little sister's arm and tried to drag her off her seat. Esther placed her small hands on the bottom of her chair and held on tight. Malka was bigger and stronger. She pulled Esther away, raising her voice in her loud and bossy way. By now, Esther was crying.

Leah looked at her mother, then her father, hoping one of them would do something. She was surprised none of the grown-ups said anything.

"You can eat with us another time," Leah said. "We'll get kosher food just for you, right Mommy?"

"We'll see," Sarah said. "I'll talk to her parents to make a plan."

After the young neighbors went downstairs, Leah's family ate without speaking. The quiet felt strange so Leah piped up, "I came home when the big hand was on the 12 and the little hand was on the six. I think I'm learning how to tell time."

13. The Detective Gets Involved

Momism: Secrets are meant to be kept.

A week after my first meeting with John, we returned to Panera. I inhaled the fragrance of fresh pastries and cursed the menu on the wall above the cashier that included calories for each selection.

After John ordered a sandwich and I chose half a Fuji apple chicken salad, we filled our coffee cups and snagged a booth toward the rear of the restaurant. Despite our pleasant beginning last time, I felt awkward. Maybe it was because I still knew so little about him. More likely, it was because our kids were dating.

After we were seated, he leaned back, arms folded across his chest, resting on his mildly protruding belly. Once again, I watched him stretch his long legs under the table. His sneakers were enormous. His gray hoodie had "NAVY" plastered on the front.

"Were you in the navy or is that an Old Navy shirt you're wearing?"

John grunted a half laugh then rubbed his eyes beneath his glasses before answering.

"I was in the Navy and the Army and the Air Force. Skipped the Coast Guard, Marine Corps and Space Force."

"I never heard of anyone joining three branches of the armed services. How did you manage it?"

"One at a time. Not the usual military path. I wanted to try three before becoming a lifer. Instead of choosing, I became a cop, then a detective."

"Impressive," I said, absorbing the goodness of this man and his career.

Kevin had made the cover of *New York* magazine as a top plastic surgeon in Manhattan. I'm so proud of my husband, though sometimes I wonder why a person who spends his days making women, and often men, look younger deserves such fame while John, who defended our country, is destined to be anonymous. It didn't feel right.

I liked the guy, but at the same time, I felt this was not the kind of family I expected my son to marry into. What was wrong with me?

I could hear my mom saying, *If ever there was a moment when you should keep your mouth closed, this is it.* I decided to shift our discussion.

"John, you called our meeting. Does that mean you're going to work on the case? I don't want to pressure you, especially since I keep vacillating. One minute I'm obsessed with the skeleton and the next, I'm completely into my boutique. Every time I push the skeleton aside, it creeps back into my brain."

"Same here. Thought I'd be fishing now that I'm retired, but I can't get the damn set of bones outta my head. I talked to my wife. She's convinced I'm already involved."

He looked directly at me and I felt as if I could hear his mind calculating options.

"Then there's your Sean and my Sophie. Teaming up will give us a chance to get acquainted, like the kids want. So, yes. I'm in," he said, then added, "that is, if you are."

"We're both in, pinkies' promise," I said reaching out my freshly manicured hand.

John smiled at my silly request then linked my pinky with his that was twice the size of my finger. He grunted his half laugh that I was getting used to.

"Nice nail color," he said. "You paint them yourself?"

"I get a manicure once a week. Why do you ask?"

"Well, it's none of my business, but Nancy pointed out that doing her own nails saved $15.00 a week if you count the added tip. Do that for 52 weeks and you spend $780 a year. Multiply that by twenty years and you come to $15,600."

"So, Nancy is the careful one," I said, both impressed and irritated. Who was this man to dump such a big criticism on how I spend my money? Now I didn't like him and I didn't want to hear what he had to say.

"Moving on," I said, hiding my hands in my lap. "Will we visit your buddies at the police station?"

"They don't want me there. That's the formal position. Of course, I'll work around it."

"Okay," I said as I picked on my 270-calorie lunch. "What does work around it mean?"

"It means we need to gather our own info. First off, I want to see the forensics report. It's amazing how much information science can provide about what happened long ago."

"Isn't the forensic report only available to the police?"

"That's what I'll work around. My buddies will share, but not officially. Once I see that information, we might know if we have a crime."

"Of course we have a crime."

"Can't assume that. Maybe the person fell in."

"Maybe the person was pushed, or killed and then hidden," I said.

John was quiet for a few moments.

"If the skeleton is a child, and I think it is because of its size," I said, tapping my foot under the table until my shoe fell off and relieved the pressure on my bunion, "it's terrible regardless of how it happened."

"It's terrible for an adult as well."

"Can you get the report tomorrow?"

"This isn't TV. It's real life. Everything takes time. Guess you've got a lot to learn."

John's instructional attitude infuriated me. Though he was admirable, his say-it-as-I-see-it style pushed me away. I glared at him, aware of the din of other conversations, a toddler crying, the clatter of silverware as people around us ate lunch.

"Sorry. Let me rephrase that," he said, taking responsibility for the shift in mood.

"Even better, let's erase it. Nothing to be gained if we're antagonistic, right?"

I nodded, liking him again, then changed the subject. I was getting very good at changing the subject.

"Can I come with you?"

"Where?"

"To talk to people."

"Communication with my friends will be private. Just me or they won't reveal classified info. You would become a witness to their transgressions."

"So how do we work together?"

"Glad you asked. I have an idea. That's why I asked to meet you. I already have some facts that will help."

"Facts are good," I said, hoping I could find a way to enjoy working together, especially for Sean's sake. I smiled while trying to get my shoe back on under the table.

"Remember, there was a gold Star of David around the skeleton's neck. The victim probably was Jewish," John said.

"Obviously," I said, then regretted how condescending it sounded. Maybe we were both punching out to establish our value. "Is this relevant to our search?"

"Might be, might not. Don't forget, we're dealing just with bones. This had to have happened a long time ago, maybe 30, 40 or even 50 years ago."

"Meaning?"

"Meaning maybe an immigrant family was involved. There was a huge influx of Eastern European and Russian Jews in the early 20th century."

"My grandparents were part of that group. They came through Ellis Island. Later they moved to Westchester," I said.

"Many moved to Brooklyn's Crown Heights and Brownsville. Some of the wealthier ones migrated to the Upper East Side of Manhattan."

"Where my store is."

"Exactly."

"Are you saying the victim's parents, or more likely, grandparents were immigrants from Eastern Europe or Russia?"

"Statistics and the gold star lean that way."

"Why does this matter?"

"Immigrants unfamiliar with American culture often kept to themselves."

"So? I'm not following your logic."

"So, they might have avoided the police even if a crime were committed. Not sure there will be records of a missing person."

It was an unsettling idea so I shook it away, shifting the discussion yet again.

"Wearing a Star of David reminds me of Francesca wearing a cross," I said. "She cares about being Catholic."

"Who's Francesca? Sounds sexy," he said, sitting up straighter.

"My designer," I said, annoyed that just her name got a reaction from John.

"She's Italian, from Italy and yes, sexy. She reminds me of Sophia Loren. I flew her to New York to see the store before we broke down the wall. She's back in Florence but will return for the opening."

"Fancy. A bona fide Italian designer straight from Italy," John said with his half grunt laugh. "How'd you find her?"

There was my mother again, filling up my head. *You promised to keep your secret,* she said. *Remember your promise and keep your mouth closed.*

"I met her in Italy," I said.

Something about John made me feel as if he could see what I wasn't telling him. His ability to ask questions, his unrelenting eye contact and his way of listening encouraged me to blurt out personal things though he was practically a stranger. I babbled on.

"I was visiting someone in the hospital and needed an interpreter. I contacted Roberto, a waiter in the hotel I stayed at in Florence before Kevin joined me," I said, folding and unfolding my hands. "When he arrived at the hospital to translate, he developed a pain in his chest and asked me to call his wife, Francesca."

I was sorry I tumbled out this information, sure I appeared guilty of something, though I had no reason to feel guilty. Not really. The rash that suddenly appeared on my face said otherwise.

"You went alone to Italy. How did you know someone who was in a hospital?" John said, maintaining calm eye contact.

I checked my polished nails, flicked my red hair, stared at the ceiling.

"It's way too long a story to share right now," I said, guarding more details that should never be revealed.

"No problem," he said moving his feet back under his chair, getting ready to stand.

"The important fact is that I met Francesca who was wearing the most amazing red dress," I said. "She designed it herself. Her fashions inspired me to open a boutique."

"Got it," John said. "Now back to our pinky promise. It's just a hunch. Like I said last time, I think the people who lived in the upstairs apartments at the time, or whoever ran the store, could prove important. Are you willing to do some research, call the owner of the building, check records on the Internet?"

"Absolutely."

"Oh, one more thing," he said. "Nancy and I cruised to the Bahamas for our 25th anniversary. A year later, we enjoyed a bus tour in Italy. Going alone—not a chance for either one of us."

Was this his way of criticizing me again or was he simply tactless? I covered my negative reaction with a smile.

"Excuse my language," John said as he held the door open for me. "Lady, you've got balls."

14. Fall, 1954

Where was he? Everyday Grandpa walked Leah to school then picked her up at 3:00 PM when class was over. Now that she was in third grade, she had begged her parents to let her walk home alone. Her mother wouldn't allow it, so she tried her father. He shook his head no, and he was the easier one. Maybe this time they changed their mind. But wouldn't they have told her? Wouldn't someone at school have given her a message?

She waited outside the front door as the rest of the kids raced by, some meeting their mothers, others laughing in groups. She saw their neighbor pick up her children. Esther waved. They didn't stop because Leah always went home with her grandfather.

Leah looked at her new Mickey Mouse watch and saw that ten minutes had passed since school let out. Should she go home? She knew the way. What if Grandpa came late and couldn't find her? She didn't know what to do. By 3:20 it got quiet. She was alone and worried.

The school door was still open so Leah went back inside to find her teacher.

"Nobody is answering the phone, dear. I'll take you home. I'm sure everyone got busy and simply forgot what time it was."

First, they walked to Madison Avenue. At the corner, Leah looked both ways, careful to wait for a green light, knowing that crossing the street could be dangerous. As they strode downtown, Leah wanted to peak in the store windows at the colorful displays, especially the pastries at luncheonettes, but her teacher encouraged her to get home as soon as possible.

They realized something bad must have happened when they saw a large, red fire truck. As they got closer, Leah noticed police preventing cars from driving near her building. She stopped and took her teacher's hand. One cop asked where they were going, then escorted them to her mother who was standing with their neighbors looking up at their third-floor apartment.

"Oh, my goodness. Is it three o'clock already?" Sarah said as Leah ran into her mother's arms. "I've been so frantic about the fire I didn't pay attention to the time."

Usually, Leah squirmed away. This time she held on to her mother's waist.

"I can't believe we forgot all about you," her mother said while kissing the top of her head. "I'm so, so sorry. Thank God you're okay. And let's give a special thank-you to your teacher for bringing you home!"

Leah looked around. Grandma was sitting on the curb, her head in her hands with Grandpa's arm around her. Their neighbor also was outside, holding her broom, her six kids huddled nearby watching the firemen. Malka sneered as Esther got up and moved closer to Leah.

"What happened?" Leah asked her mother. "Is Grandpa all right? When he didn't come to school, I thought something was wrong with him."

"Grandpa's fine. We had a little fire in the kitchen. Everything is okay now."

"A fire?" Leah said, no longer able to hold back tears. "Oh, Mommy! I'm scared of so many things," she said between sobs, "I never thought to be scared of a fire."

"The important thing to remember is that everyone is safe. Can you remember that? We're all safe. The fire was caught early and we're going to be all right."

"Were you with Grandma?"

"No, dear. I was downstairs in the grocery store. When the fire broke out, Grandpa grabbed Grandma and raced downstairs, pounding on our neighbor's door on their way. Then Grandpa found the fire alarm box and called for help. He's our hero."

"Does Daddy know?"

"I called him at work. He'll be here soon. Aunt Dina, too."

Leah stopped crying and tried to make sense of what she saw. A hose was inside the open front door, long enough to go up the stairs. She didn't see flames like in a big fire she once saw in a scary movie. Maybe only one fire truck was a good sign.

Just then, Leah saw Aunt Dina and cousin Rachel.

"Smoke is floating out from the living room window," Dina said.

"It looks like we have more smoke than anything else," Sarah told them.

"How did it happen?"

"Grandma was cooking. She was roasting a chicken in the oven and heating up some soup with *matzo* balls on the stove," Sarah said. "When the chicken was done, she took it out of the oven and forgot to shut the flame under the soup. She's been forgetting many things lately."

"So, Grandma started the fire?" Dina said.

"It looks like it. She said the soup evaporated and the empty pot charred. She smelled it and tried to remove the pot with a dishtowel."

"So far it's all logical. I dread hearing what's next," Dina said.

"She told me the flame was still on and the towel caught on fire. It was hot and close to her body so she threw it away and it hit the lace curtains. They must have burst into flames quickly."

"Poor Grandma," Rachel said as she listened to the adults.

"It smells out here," Leah said. "Did my new science book burn, the one with the pictures of all the parts inside a body? The one Daddy bought me. Is it okay?"

"I don't know. We're not allowed upstairs yet."

By this time, Leah's dad appeared. He kissed Sarah then took his daughter in one arm and put the other arm around Esther who was hovering close by.

"I'll get you another book," he said. "Be glad nobody was hurt."

The fire did not spread out of the kitchen so it didn't take long for the firemen to complete their work. After they did a walk-through to determine it was okay for the family to return, Leah's parents went in first. It seemed like a week before they came out, shaking their heads. Sarah was biting her bottom lip.

"Well?" Dina said.

"I'm not sure. It looks like more water damage than anything else. And the whole place reeks. The kitchen's a mess. Some of the walls were seared. The one near the window is exposed. The linoleum floor is fire resistant, though I think I saw a few burn marks and melted spots. It's worse in one small area, also near the window. There's so much water. Some probably leaked into the downstairs apartment."

"OOOh, Mommy," Leah said. "That's gonna make Esther's mother so mad. And Malka, too."

"I know, dear. It's a good thing Daddy insisted we buy insurance. We'll fix her ceiling. Maybe she'll stop banging it with her broom every time we make noise. We'll also be able to repair the room and replace our things."

"What things, Mommy? What got spoiled?"

"You always want to know everything, *Bubala*. The legs of our Formica table where we eat every day are partially gone. So are the wooden chairs. What's left is blackened. The dining room stuff also smells but doesn't look bad. The firemen soaked the living room."

"What about your brocade burgundy chairs and mahogany table," said Dina, "and your beautiful oriental carpet?"

"Also damaged," Sarah said.

"Not those things, Mommy. I mean the things in our rooms—my stuffed animals and my dresses with the pockets and my Mary Jane shoes. Can we sleep here tonight or do we have to stay with Aunt Dina?"

"One thing at a time."

"What about my room?"

"Your bedroom, my bedroom and the bathroom in the back of the apartment are in good shape—except for the odor and dribbles of water on the floor that ran in from the kitchen. Most of all we have to air everything out."

"Can I go see? Please can I go see? I promise I'll be careful."

"Absolutely not," her mother said, then turned to Dina. "It might be smart to stay with you for at least a night or two. We'll need to repair one wall as well as invest in a complete paint job in the kitchen. Whatever happens, I doubt I'll be able to do Thanksgiving next month. Maybe I can take over the Passover Seder instead."

"I can't believe you're thinking so far ahead. Of course I'll switch," Dina said while patting her sister's hand. "Guess my soft-spoken sister is tougher than she sounds. Maybe Rachel will get stronger as she grows up, become more like you."

By this time, the fire truck had left and the neighbors had gone back to their apartments. Grandma refused to get up from the curb.

"It's all her fault," Leah said to her cousin as she pointed to Grandma.

"Why can't you be nicer to her? She didn't mean to start a fire," Rachel said.

"Why are you always taking her side?" Leah said.

"She's the only one who can get the knots out of my hair when I wash it. And she never says anything about my weight. She's smart, too. She taught your daddy how to drive a car. Did you know that?"

Leah shook her head and kept quiet.

"Grandma, we still love you," Rachel said while rubbing her grandmother's back.

"*Oy*, my head is *tsedrait*. My *kop* is *tsemisht*."

"It's okay if your head got mixed up," Rachel said. "When you make a mistake, that's how you learn. Remember? That's what you always tell me."

"When I grow up, I'm going to be a doctor," Leah said. "Then I can help you so your head won't be mixed up."

"A doctor? Better you should *marry* a doctor," Grandma said. "Better you should stay home and take care of your babies."

"Daddy says I can do both. He thinks soon everyone will have a job. And Mommy worked. She was a model before she had me."

"Vat does your daddy know? He doesn't like Shabbat. He doesn't go to synagogue. He vorks in his drug store all day and den he vorks some more and falls asleep in the middle of family dinners."

"Leah, leave Grandma alone," Dina said. "This isn't the time to have an argument. You just had a fire and we need to concentrate on what to do next."

Leah ignored her aunt.

"My daddy knows how to swim. He promised to teach me next summer just like he taught me to ride a bike," Leah said.

"Dat vas *gut*. Maybe he can find you a husband before you are twenty-von so you don't have to vork."

"Aunt Dina does both. She has Rachel and a hotel and you even help in the kitchen."

"Aunt Dina married a handsome lawyer. Rich. He bought her the hotel. Dat's how she got her vork. And she doesn't need it."

"Well, I already have a job."

"Vat job, *Bubala*? Vat are you talking about?"

"My job is to study and do well at school. Daddy pays me a silver dollar for each Satisfactory or A that I get on my report card. Those are the two best grades. Last year I had five subjects and four report cards. I have nineteen silver dollars. One time I got a B in penmanship and had to work extra hard to do better. And I don't do so well in listening, but Daddy doesn't care."

"*Abi gezunt.* As long as you're healthy."

"Enough, already, Leah," Dina said. "We need to figure out what to do right here, right now, not worry about when you'll marry."

"I'm still gonna be a doctor, and you can't stop me," Leah said to her grandmother.

Then, without asking permission, she turned around, grabbed Esther's hand and together they ran into the building and up the two flights of stairs that led straight to their dining room. Rachel looked at her mother who nodded yes. She followed her cousin.

Inside, the three girls saw that Grandma and Grandpa's room to the left of the steps was untouched. The ornate mahogany furniture looked as regal as before and the mauve flat bedspread remained neatly placed on the double bed. As they tiptoed into the kitchen, they crinkled their noses from the odor.

"I wonder how long we'll have this smell," Leah said.

"Maybe you'll get used to it, like when you don't know your clothes smell terrible because you wear them too long, but Mommy knows."

"It's not so bad. It reminds me of roasting s'mores with the Brownies when we made a campfire in Van Cortlandt Park."

"Bet your parents won't agree. Let's go check your room."

While Rachel ran to the back of the apartment, Leah raced to what was once a laundry chute that led to the ground floor. The landlord had installed a floor, then hid the shaft behind a locked door. When Leah jiggled the knob, the door always sprang open. That's where she kept her silver dollars, in one of her mother's shoe bags. When Leah hid there, she was very careful to avoid the hole that still existed in the back. There was enough room in the closet for her to stand. Even an adult could squeeze in. This was her favorite hiding place because nobody in the family ever used the chute. Leah opened the closet even though Esther was sticking close by. When she took a quick look, Esther tried to wiggle inside.

"Stand back. There's a magic spirit in there," Leah said, hoping to scare her younger neighbor away.

"I want to see it," Esther said.

"Only kidding."

The little girl started to cry.

"Hurry and take a look," she said to Esther, grabbing her hand so she wouldn't get hurt.

"I can't see the magic spirit," Esther said.

"I told you I was kidding. There's no magic spirit."

"Is too, and you won't show it to me. You're being mean, like Malka."

"Where are you?" Rachel yelled from another room.

"We have to leave," Leah said, pulling Esther toward the stairs.

"There's too much smoke," her cousin said. "It's making me cough. Meet me at the front door."

"We're coming," Leah said, relieved that her secret place was untouched by flames or water and her 19 silver dollars were safe.

15. A Change of Direction

Momism: Finish what you start.

"Susan, what are you going to do with the people calling my office about the skeleton?" Kevin said, while carrying a glass of chardonnay and a Macallan on the rocks down the hall to join me in the living room. "Don't you want to call them back?"

"I can't, Kev. Their stories are too horrific. So many missing people, so many tragedies. All the years I've been having fun, creating good images for the ad agency, I've ignored the less fortunate. I feel so shallow."

"Come on, honey," he said, sitting next to me on the couch and putting his drink on the white marble coaster I placed on the coffee table.

Max joined us, plopping down in front of Kevin.

"That's nonsense. You're acting like you live in a bubble. You've always been aware of peoples' misfortunes and done your share to help. You donate to charities."

"When you have money, that's easy. I keep wondering what the skeleton's family must feel."

You know what they feel, said my mother. *Concentrate on your feelings.*

"I cry because I don't have answers the callers are looking for," I said between sips of my chilled white wine. "There's too much sadness."

"I think you're looking for an excuse to back away. It's not like you to leave something unfinished. The people phoning my office want you, not me. You need a response plan."

"It's not as simple as I thought," I said, slipping off my heels and freeing my stocking feet to let my toes enjoy the plush Oriental rug. "I no longer have the stomach to be in the middle of a cold case that obviously happened years ago and has nothing to do with me."

"You're flip flopping again. Unfortunately, the bones were found in your store so like it or not, you have to deal with it. On the upside, every time the press mentions the skeleton, they mention *Susanna's*."

"Oh yes, the media. They used to be my friends. Now they hound me. I have no privacy. I wish they'd leave me alone."

Susan, when you talk to them, remember this has nothing to do with your life, your history, my mother said. *And make sure to get your hair done.*

Kevin looked at me with his "I know what you're thinking" look. Does that come with all long marriages? It makes me feel linked to him. We sat, lost in our own thoughts, while Joshua Bell played the violin on our old-fashioned stereo the kids tried to replace more than once.

"Okay, of course I want publicity for my new venture," I said, moving my feet to his lap. "Despite my years in business, I'm not sure I can shift media attention from the person in the wall. Discussing old bones is much juicier than a new hemline or fabric, no matter how chic."

"I have great faith you'll find a way to use your skills to cover both situations," Kevin said, then retrieved the bottle of wine to refill my glass.

"I can't tolerate another reporter asking me my thoughts about the skeleton. Right now, I just want to open my boutique."

By now, Kevin was back on the couch putting his arm around me. Instinctively, I cuddled up.

"I hope a few fashion editors will come to the opening as well as a broadcast network or two."

"Less than a minute ago you were committed to bringing peace of mind to the child's relatives. Did I miss something? What just happened?"

"What happened? The police refuse to talk to me and my two fruitless meetings with Sophie's dad is what happened."

"I thought you liked John."

"Most of the time, I do, despite our differences. Sometimes his honesty hurts, though I appreciate that he's so genuine. It's refreshing, but as far as the case is concerned, we're still no closer to knowing anything."

My attention returned to the store, then to Francesca and Roberto, who claimed he couldn't attend the event because he's unable to change shifts at work. A waiter, unable to change his schedule. Give me a break.

I don't care if it's a fabricated excuse. I'm relieved he won't be here. If Roberto does come, I already convinced Kevin to put them up in a hotel, afraid I would blush or be tense every time we were in the same room.

Even without Roberto, the guest list to attend the opening was starting to get as complicated as a wedding.

Kevin would take the day off. Both my kids confirmed they were coming as expected, though Jennifer's husband couldn't get there until the end of the party.

When Sean told me he was bringing Sophie, a double dose of anxiety exploded. I had hoped we could meet before the event, and have a chance to chat. The only option my son offered was to go to dinner after the cocktail party.

"You know, classes and rounds, Mom," he said. "We have so little time."

Of course, I had to invite Sophie's dad, which meant I'd have to invite her mother, Nancy, whom I also haven't met. I bet they'd prefer a beer to prosecco. I didn't dare tell John to ditch his Navy sweatshirt and dress up, not wear sneakers. Then again, sneakers have become trendier. I tried to stop myself from being judgmental.

"Let's go look at the store," I said. "Then we'll come back and I'll cook spaghetti ala vodka with some broccoli. We can pick up cherry tomatoes and cream on the way home."

"Sounds perfect. And speaking of perfect, hiring your own photographer is a brilliant idea."

"I'll be able to provide great shots of Francesca's designs and of the people at the party instead of visions of a crime scene. I'm also inviting the press to come an hour early. That way I can answer questions."

"Now, you're talking like the Susan I know."

"Wait'll you see the store. It looks dynamite, especially the orange loveseat Francesca suggested. It's absolutely smashing in back near two pale gray chairs. I decided to have racks for blouses and pants line one wall. Another rack on the other wall holds dresses. The center contains showcases for small bags, scarves and costume jewelry. The lighting is perfect. I love it."

"Who's coming?"

"I'm not sure yet. We invited some friends from our building, people who are on the Board with you. Jennifer asked lots of coworkers from her office and from her high school days at Dalton."

"I'm glad you'll have different ages at the party. Makes the place seem more vibrant."

"I included some associates from my old ad agency, from my tennis group, my Pilates class and the owners of the dance studio where we take lessons. It'll be like a mini reunion. Most promised to bring their friends."

"We still have some time so I'll add some doctors and their wives. The more big-spenders, the better."

"Right, but our prices aren't crazy. Pants are all under $1,000 and silk blouses are less. We'll have a few items under $200, mostly costume jewelry, scarves and belts to complete the basics."

"You're kidding yourself. Even my Juvederm ladies might think your merchandise is pricey," Kevin said, "though I think you'll pull in the designer crowd and they can handle the cost."

"If we have perfect May weather," I said, ignoring his comment about costs, "I can keep the doors open. By starting at 5:00 we'll be able to capture some Upper East Siders walking home from work or picking up their kids from ballet or soccer. Baby strollers and large dogs will have to stay outside."

"You're well organized."

"Yep," I said, proudly.

"So, you have some free time to respond to all the people calling my office," Kevin said, circling back to our original conversation. "Listen to today's list. There's a Michael Conway who says his son is the skeleton. A Maria Alfonsinetti insists it's her sister. A strange man says he hid his daughter in the wall and is ready to confess. That one should go to the police."

"They should all go to the police."

"Oh, and someone named Leah called three times. She wants to meet with you. She didn't leave her last name or any additional information. Just Leah."

"I'm not calling any of them. I don't believe I can help them and I don't want to hear their stories."

"Maybe one of them can help you find the answers you were looking for just a few hours ago. I don't care if you keep flip flopping about your interest level. I do care about how we're going to field these calls."

"Honey, you're not listening. I'm done. It's time to get back to the world of fashion. I'm not calling anyone—not Michael, not Maria and not Leah."

16. December, 1954

"Is Mama there?" Sarah asked Dina, talking into the handle of her black dial phone. "Please dear God, let her be with you."

"She's not here," Dina said. "Maybe she's with Papa on one of his walks. They both love to go out for a piece of cake or apple pie and a glass of hot tea in the afternoon. You know how he enjoys sucking on a cube of sugar while his drink cools."

Sarah shook her head though Dina couldn't see her.

"Papa's right here. He's getting ready to pick up Leah from school. He wants me to call the police," Sarah said, "but it's only been a few hours."

"What are you going to tell them? Our sixty-five-year-old mother has gone out and you want them to find her?"

Sarah was tired. If her mother wasn't telling her what to do, then her older sister was bossing her around. She felt she was always the one to cave in.

"What's wrong with involving the police?" Sarah said with a dramatic sigh.

"First of all, Mama hasn't been away long enough for them to take action. Second, she'll freak out if an officer approaches her. She'll start screaming in Russian about pogroms. It could get ugly. Don't call the police."

Once again, Dina acted as if she knew everything, as if she were smarter. Maybe she was, though she had quit school after eighth grade while Sarah had earned a high school diploma. Sometimes living so close was a challenge rather than a joy.

Then there was the sisterly competition. Sarah was prettier. Even if her blonde hair was pulled back in a simple ponytail, she outshined Dina who tried harder, always wore the latest fashions and changed the style of her dark brown hair to match what she saw in magazines. She let everyone know she was a business woman, running a hotel in the mountains each summer.

"Ugly and safe is better than wandering around out of her mind," Sarah said, sitting at the kitchen table. "We don't know where she is and I don't know where to look. She left the door to the apartment wide open. She's not thinking clearly."

"If she's out of the house, at least she's not telling you how to live."

"Dina, that's horrible," Sarah said, knowing her sister had hit a raw spot. As long as Mama was confused and vulnerable, Sarah felt a little relief, a slight bit of freedom from the choking hold her mother had on her. It was hard to admit.

"Okay, that was harsh," Dina said.

"I'm the one who yields during arguments while you manage to sort things out the way you want," Sarah said. "Mama is missing again. It's serious."

"Exactly how long has she been gone this time?"

Before Sarah could answer, the doorbell rang.

"Just a minute, there's someone here. I'll call you right back."

Upon opening the door, Sarah faced one of their neighbors who lived in the next building. She was standing with Mama who was dressed in her housecoat and apron rather than one of her elegant going-out suits. Sarah gave her mother a tight hug, holding on with her eyes closed until her mother pulled away.

"I saw your mother walking along Madison Avenue by herself. It's cold out and she wasn't wearing a coat," the neighbor said. "She appeared a little confused, stopping to stare up at the buildings in all directions, then moving in circles."

"Thank you," Sarah said, while Papa put his arms around his wife. "Thank you so much."

"She didn't remember my name," the neighbor said. "I offered to walk her home. At first, she mumbled something about a chicken—should she cook it or keep it to lay eggs. I asked her where she kept her chicken. She didn't answer, seemingly in her own world. Then she became like a lost child, happy to have someone lead her home."

"My *shayna maidel*, vee didn't know you left. Vhere vere you going?" Papa said.

"For a valk. Den I didn't remember how to get back."

Sarah called her sister again, not knowing what to do. Should they consult a doctor or the community rabbi? Sarah knew many people sought a rabbi's advice, but that wasn't her way.

"You can't be with Mama all the time. You're going to need some help," Dina said. "I can't do much with Rachel so sick. She's coughing far more often and has fever. I tried Mama's mustard plaster. It isn't working. We're taking her to a doctor. I won't leave her alone until she starts to improve."

"Don't worry about us," Sarah said. "Papa is with Mama most of the time. Every morning, after he drops Leah off at school, he likes to get the newspaper and have a coffee over on 86th Street. When he tries to include Mama, she says she prefers to stay home and work in the kitchen. Even during her confused moments, she knows where she keeps her apron and puts it on."

"I thought she isn't allowed to cook since the fire."

"She can help as long as I'm there. If we take away everything Mama likes to do, I'm afraid she'll get depressed. She's already scared she's losing her mind."

"Well, she is, isn't she?"

"Aren't you being too tough?"

"Sometimes the truth is tough."

"I guess. I pretend each incident is an isolated event. After a moment of forgetfulness, she bounces back. She still records every penny we spend for food, electricity, heat, even what Solly spends on gas for the car. She makes Papa go to different stores to get the best price on groceries so there's something left over to save for Rachel and Leah to go to college. She's lucid enough to know she's not always there. She knows she's failing."

"Now that you bought your own TV, maybe she can enjoy watching more shows. It'll keep her busy and safe."

"She's already glued to the TV at night. During the day she alternates between being the Mama we know and mumbling about when she was a young girl. Yesterday she sounded like she was talking to someone in Yiddish. Nobody was with her. It's sad and creepy at the same time," Sarah said.

The sisters continued their discussion, elaborating the obvious, circling back to the same questions.

"Does she always mutter something strange before she gets confused?" Dina said.

"I don't know. I'll have to pay better attention," Sarah said, wondering why she hadn't thought of that.

"What if she leaves again?"

"I'm sure she'll try. Last time she left, I told Papa I plan to install a locked gate at the top of the stairs. I'll have to hide the key even though it'll be inconvenient for all of us. I'll stick it in a plant by the door."

"What about Leah? If you call it a job and pay her, she might help."

"I love Leah, but we all know she does what she wants. More than once, I wished I had her strength. Part of me admires the way she bucks me. When Leah heard about the gate, she announced she'd climb over without needing the key. Let's hope Mama doesn't watch her and try the same thing."

For a few days, everything was back to normal. The family gathered in the evenings to watch *Milton Berle*, *I Love Lucy* or *The Ed Sullivan Show*. Leah curled up in her father's lap, though he was still wearing his suit and tie. Grandpa enjoyed another glass of tea. Mama and Sarah got to relax. Then the problem surfaced again.

"Mama went roaming last night," Sarah said to Dina. "One minute she was sleeping next to Papa. When he went to put his arm around her, he noticed she wasn't there."

"She came back, right?" Dina said.

"Not by herself. This time the rabbi found her. She was in her nightgown. No robe. No sweater. No coat, despite the cold. Just the long white cotton gown she was wearing when she went to bed."

"How did the rabbi get to her?"

"He was returning from a wedding at the shul. I guess once Mama got outside, she heard the music down the block and walked toward the synagogue, I assume to join the dancing. I can just picture her marching right up to a table, grabbing two spoons and clicking them together in time to the music. This is the third time this month she's strayed."

"I think you have to call a doctor," Dina said.

"What for? It's our problem and there is no medication."

"You sound like you caught Mama's fear of the establishment."

"I'm telling you right now, I'm not putting her in a home. She's only sixty-five and besides, Papa would be lost without her."

"Did I say anything about a home?"

"No, not yet, though I've thought of it." Sarah said. "I bet you have, too. Maybe Mama needs to wear a bell to alert us when she leaves. And a necklace with her name and address engraved on it."

While the sisters continued to discuss the situation, Mama sat down at the kitchen table.

"I vant you should feed the chickens today. I'm too tired."

"What chickens, Mama? What are you talking about?" Sarah said, still holding the phone.

"Mama is confused," Dina could be heard shouting. "Watch her today. Maybe this means she'll soon try to leave. It could be a pattern," Dina said before hanging up.

"Mama, we don't have live chickens. We're in Manhattan," Sarah said.

Her mother didn't react. It was as if she were in another world and didn't hear her daughter.

"A fox ate von of our chickens. He vill come for more. Den vee vill not have eggs. Vee vill not have anyting to sell in the market. Vat should vee do?" she said, as she put her head in her hands. "Vee don't have money for a good fence and the fox dug a hole to get into the coop. I must find the rabbi. He vill tell me vat to do. I must go before it gets dark."

Sarah watched her mother get up, fetch her handbag from her bedroom and return to the kitchen. For a few minutes she sat at the new Formica table then opened the refrigerator, counted the eggs and rushed to the front door. Sarah followed.

Outside, Mama strolled in the sunshine along the wide cement sidewalk toward the synagogue.

Though it was early afternoon, midweek, the lights were on. Some workers were washing the front windows where anti-Semitic slogans had been painted. It was the second time this month.

Once inside, Sarah could see prayer books in slots behind each maple wood bench. Plaques on the back of seats commemorated departed loved ones. Despite high ceilings and continuous cleaning, a musty smell lingered.

Nobody except Mama was in the sanctuary. Maybe the rabbi was in his office. Everyone knew he often took his children with him to do their homework while he worked on his next sermon.

Mama turned, saw Sarah, and smiled.

"I guess I vent for von of my valks. Vee can go home now," Mama said, as if everything were normal.

Sarah shivered, bracing for more similar incidents.

17. Here Comes Francesca

Momism: Shake your sins of the past.

"Hi, hon," Kevin said on his way back to our apartment from JFK. He had taken the silver Mercedes rather than the black Porsche 911 convertible to have more room. "Francesca's in the car and she brought a wonderful surprise."

It was one week before we opened and my designer had flown to New York from Italy to help places clothes in the windows and enjoy the introductory party in the store.

"I love surprises. Can you tell me what it is?" I said, knowing my voice was on speaker and she could hear me.

"Sure can." His tone meant he was smiling. "Roberto."

"Roberto," I said, without a smile in my voice. "What do you mean 'Roberto'?"

"*Ciao, mon ami,*" Roberto said. "*Sono molto felice,* how you say—happy to be here. I am happy you let your light shine out. I am happy for you and Francesca."

"Happy, happy," I mumbled, thinking about his knack of dispensing gobbledygook. How would I put up with his shining nonsense and psychobabble for an entire week? For sure, they weren't staying in Jennifer's old bedroom as originally planned for Francesca. I needed to get off the phone and make a hotel reservation for them before they got to our apartment. He better not start in on my aura and my radiance in front of Kevin.

He does have a point, Mom said. *You developed a wonderful glow, a real sparkle since your trip to Europe.*

Despite my lack of interest in Roberto, I found myself in front of a full-length mirror in the bigger of my two walk-in closets. I refreshed my chocolate brown eyeliner and fixed my hair that I had already fixed. I changed into a fresh white silk blouse and traded my jeans for black crepe slacks then padded to the living room to pour a glass of vodka on the rocks, assuming it looked like I was drinking water.

Of course, they arrived in what felt like a nano second. Should I kiss him hello on both cheeks as is the custom in Italy or would we shake hands? That seemed way too formal. As I opened the door, I decided to make no decisions.

Francesca entered first, giving me air pecks on both sides of my face. As usual, she looked stunning. Today she wore a black suit with a low-cut red blouse under an open short jacket. A Ferragamo red and black silk scarf was tied to the handle of her handbag. Pretty expensive considering her husband was a waiter. I was amazed she could be so polished after sitting in a plane for hours and didn't understand why her husband needed other women to fulfill his life.

"*Ciao, Susanna,*" Roberto said, as he threw his arms around me in a bear hug. I stood stiffly, my hands at my sides, not quite in the pockets of my pants.

Kevin rolled his eyes, then rallied. Ever the perfect host, he left the suitcases in our entrance hall under our Miro signed print, a splash of color in our white and gray apartment, then escorted our guests into the living room. Joining them, I tripped and spilled some of my drink on the couch, grateful it was a clear liquid. Roberto immediately pulled out a handkerchief and mopped up my mess. Kevin didn't say a word. His eyes acknowledged he took it all in.

I thought of the time Roberto did the same in the breakfast room at the Westin Excelsior Hotel when I knocked over a small vase of flowers on the table. Damn those handkerchiefs. Maybe Robert's silver-fox good looks made me jumpy. It was going to be a very long week.

Remember, Susan, if you can't change what's happening, change your attitude, Mom said. *A long week is only seven short days.*

"Roberto's English is excellent," Kevin said. "It's good he's here. He can help translate for Francesca." Then Kevin leaned in to whisper in my ear.

"Most of the time I don't know what he's talking about. On the ride here, he was commenting on the setting sun, the light it shined on trees, buildings, even the street. Then he added something about people not knowing how much they have to offer until their light goes on inside. What kind of crap is that?"

I shrugged my shoulders as if I had no idea. It was best Kevin didn't know that for a brief instant in Florence, I had enjoyed Roberto's philosophy. If my husband had any inkling how far I had gone with this man, he never let on. He never asked questions. Perhaps he felt that anything risqué outside our marriage did not fit my character. It's true. Except for that one moment, a terrible secret that shouldn't count. It was time to stop thinking and engage in small talk.

"How was your flight?"

"*Bene.* Ah, *che bellissimo appartamento.* What a beautiful apartment. My wife, she likes your painting, and your dog *e bello,*" Roberto said as Max nuzzled his leg.

"His name is Max. Another child in our family."

I was running out of patience with the chatter, ready to make a plan.

"It's 5:00 here. For you it's 11:00 PM. You both must be exhausted. When I heard you were here, Roberto, I took the liberty of getting you both a hotel room. I'm sure you will be more comfortable there than in our spare room. Kevin will take you to freshen up and maybe grab a nap. We'll pick you up at 8:00 to go to dinner."

"Yes," they said simultaneously.

I was glad she said something in English, even if it were just one word. I hoped it was a sign that others would come as she became more comfortable. Then they put their heads together and whispered something I couldn't hear.

"*Susanna,* Francesca is tired," Roberto said. "She wants to meet in the morning. We get taxi to the hotel. One suitcase has new dresses for the windows. We take?" he said, looking at Kevin. "Is better to stay here, yes?"

Kevin lifted the canvas bag to test how heavy it was.

"Better leave it here. We'll bring it to the store tomorrow," he said as he ushered our guests toward the hallway then turned back to me. "I'll go with them in a cab to check them into the hotel, but what's this *Susanna* business? He has a pet name for you? Did he name your store?"

"Well, yes, and no," I said, feeling my face flush with that damn red rash. "He does call me *Susanna*, but I was the one who named my store. It sounds like me, only Italian. Don't you think it fits?"

"I guess. When did this waiter have time to give you a nickname?"

I brushed away Kevin's question as if it were too silly to acknowledge while the three of them moved to the elevator in the hall.

By ten the next morning, I was in my store while Kevin went to get our guests. It was curious that Sophie's dad also showed up. He wore a blue sweater that made his incredible blue eyes quite alluring. Big improvement over his sweatshirt. At our last meeting I had told him Francesca was coming back to New York. I sensed a connection and felt life becoming more complicated.

Put on your 'I can do everything and everything is fine' face, Mom said.

This time, I took her advice and enjoyed watching John tower over Roberto when they shook hands. Then John bent down to kiss Francesca on both cheeks. I was surprised he knew the Italian custom and wondered if Roberto saw the excitement in John's eyes. Not my problem. I was glad Jennifer arrived unexpectedly.

"Mom, I have a great idea for your opening. I took the morning off to tell you in person and help organize it if you agree."

She walked over to say hello to Francesca and introduce herself to Roberto. I heard him say, *piacere,* pleased to meet you, as he kissed her hand.

"Francesca's husband is movie star gorgeous," Jennifer whispered.

"Yes, pure Rossano Brazzi."

"Who?"

"Rossano Brazzi. Before your time. Check out the classic film, *Three Coins in the Fountain.* What's your idea?"

"Mom, your opening is May 18, less than a week away. By coincidence, May 25 is National Missing Children's Day established by President Reagan. I googled it and it's also International Missing Children's Day."

"Interesting. You want me to acknowledge this somehow."

"Absolutely. You can announce you'll donate a percentage of the price of every child's outfit you sell over the next year to Find My Child."

"We don't sell children's clothing."

"You will," she said, sounding like me. "Start with a burgundy dress, one that matches the fabric found in the wall. Put it on a hanger in that smaller window that's been giving you so much creative trouble."

"We don't know if it is a child or if it's a male or female."

"So, add a second outfit for a boy."

"Fantastic idea. Tell me about the charity."

"They help find missing kids and try to prevent abductions."

"Brilliant. It will give us a solid base to connect the skeleton to life and might do some good for other families. Are you sure it's legit?"

"Mom, it's more than legit. It's amazing. Its founder was inducted into the National Women's Hall of Fame. It puts a positive spin on everything."

"I'd love to help other families, though I'm sure there will be people who criticize us for exploiting the skeleton."

"It doesn't matter, Mom. It's about the good we can start to accomplish. That's what counts."

The concept resonated with me and I decided to share it with Francesca who was leaning into John, deep in conversation.

"Can you create a little girl's dress and matching outfit for a boy?" I said.

"*Si. E possibile!*"

"Can you do it quickly, like in the next day or two?"

"*Si*," she said, nodding her head and smiling.

"Jen, this will give the media a beautiful visual to cover the story," I said. "And we'll donate 100% of the profit of the sale of the two children's ensembles."

"Why not auction them off?" Jennifer said. "You might get more interest and more money for the charity."

"Well done, Jen!" I said, patting her on the shoulder.

Jennifer's face lit up at my praise. Roberto scooted over to see what we were discussing.

"Ah, Jennifer. You have the same aura, the same inner radiance as *Susanna*," he said. "You are very lucky."

Jennifer looked at me. Her expression was impossible to interpret.

"His English is good," she whispered, "but what's he talking about? Why does he call you *Susanna*? He's such a flirt. Doesn't his wife get upset?"

"Apparently not," I said, watching Francesca lean into John again. I couldn't decipher what she was telling him, probably in a mixture of broken English and Italian. I noticed she was way more talkative than she had been with Kevin or me.

"Mom, there's someone by the window watching us. He looks kind of creepy."

The man entered the store smelling as if he had not showered in days.

"That skeleton," he said, without any introduction. "It's my dog. I want the bones to bury in my backyard."

Jennifer clenched my hand. I tried not to register any reaction. The guy looked like he couldn't afford a house with a backyard, but one never knew just by looking at someone.

John came over to help us out.

"The police have the bones," he said. "You should contact them if you have information. What's your name?"

The man left abruptly, shaking his head no. We locked the door so we could continue to work uninterrupted.

"Mom," Jennifer said. "There's another person staring at the window. She looks elegant. She's probably a future customer. Should we invite her in?"

A slim, dark-haired older woman was watching us through the glass. She stood for quite a few minutes, not moving. I couldn't stop myself from staring back. Her charcoal-grey pencil skirt fell an inch below her knees. Sheer black stockings covered her legs that would have looked sexy had she been wearing stylish heels instead of walking shoes. Her pale grey silk blouse looked expensive. We unlocked the door and waved. After a few seconds, she came inside.

"Excuse me. Are you the owner of this store?" the woman said.

"Yes," I said, with a welcoming smile, recognizing a rose fragrance, perhaps Giorgio Armani's Sky di Gioia. "We're not open yet. If you come back next week you might find something you like and you can enjoy a glass of prosecco at our party."

"Thank you. I'm more interested in the skeleton in your wall. The one written up in the papers and shown on TV."

I had expected visitors, though something about this woman made me fear what would come next. I imagined a sinister air had followed her into the boutique along with the delightful scent of roses. If this were a movie there would be chaotic unnerving music in the background.

Susan, there's no sinister air, Mom said. *You're not in a movie and you're letting your mind run wild.*

The woman looked down at her feet, appearing nervous, yet determined. Then she raised her face and our eyes met.

"I used to live in this building, many years ago, when I was a little girl."

"Oh my God," I said, clutching Jennifer's hand. I was flush with emotions I couldn't identify, hoping she was real and not some crazy person.

"My cousin, Rachel, lived around the corner," the woman said. "She used to come to my apartment after school. We both wore the same necklace that appeared in the newspaper."

She reached inside the top of her round-neck blouse to pull out a gold chain with a Star of David.

"Another family lived below us. They had six kids. Their two daughters also wore the same necklace. Most of the little girls who belonged to our neighborhood synagogue wore one."

I looked at her jewelry and gasped, then yelled. "OMG, it's the SAME necklace that was found on the skeleton in the wall!"

By now, we were all standing together. Kevin could see I was shaking and put his arm around my waist. I desperately wanted to know the lady's story. I guess we all did. So many people surrounding her must have been overwhelming. She was holding on to a nearby rack where I planned to place blouses.

"Who are you?" I said.

"My name is Leah. Dr. Leah Epstein. I can't stay. I'm a pulmonary specialist over at Mount Sinai Hospital and I have an appointment. I think I know who's in the wall," she said, almost in a whisper. "Can we meet another day? Soon?"

"No! I mean you can't leave. We have to talk now."

"My meeting is with a patient so I must go," she said, scanning the newly painted white walls and glossy molding that gleamed.

"I've avoided coming here for sixty years. Too many memories. Mostly good, but the bad ones are so terrible, I've been reluctant to face them."

"If you know who's in the wall, why not go to the police?" John said.

"I shall. First, I want to talk to you—in this store. The place is different, fresher, hopeful. As I expected, there have been many changes over the years. Despite the cosmetic differences, I still feel the original environment and that is very difficult."

I wanted to remind her that everything changes, but she was a stranger. It was not appropriate to get into a philosophical discussion. Besides, I needed facts. And I wanted them immediately. If she knew who the skeleton was, it meant the publicity worked faster than working with a detective. Score one for my old profession.

Everything is not a competition, my mother said. *If you want to find peace, it's time to stop measuring and comparing.*

"Please don't make us wait a minute longer than necessary," I said. "We open in less than a week. Though there's much to do, I'll carve a space for you. Can't you tell me more right now?"

"My story is long. It can't be rushed. I'll come back."

18. December, 1954

"I'm not getting a shot," Rachel squeezed out between sobs that escalated to a wail, drowning out the noise of cars on the street below. "I'm not going to the doctor."

"Rachel, you have fever. You're coughing. Grandma's mustard plaster and bed rest are not helping. You must have medicine," her mother said. "That's the only way to become healthy."

"Please, Mommy. Don't make me get a shot. I promise to be good. I won't even sing anymore. I'll stay in my PJs and rest. Please don't make me get a shot."

"I understand, but you need to be brave. You're my big girl. I know you can do this. I know you can be strong."

"Why doesn't the doctor give it to me here?"

"It's not one shot, dear. It's many doses over a bit of time. You'll get them at a clinic where you'll sleep and eat and be helped," Dina said, as her own tears rolled down her cheeks into the mask that was covering her nose and mouth.

"What's a clinic like?"

"It's like a hospital, only friendlier, a place where you'll get the best care from doctors who will give you all the medicine you need. You'll stay there until you're back to normal."

"Mommy! You want to send me away! To be sick all alone?"

"You won't be alone. You'll be with other children. Go back to bed and try to rest. You can read the new book I bought you."

Rachel shuffled in her slippers back to her room, whimpering while her mother fixed the crumpled sheets. Dina handed her daughter her favorite stuffed dog, tucked her into bed then closed the door, anxious to call Sarah again. The moment she heard her sister's voice, Dina's tears overflowed.

"Rachel must go to the clinic. We really have no choice. As expected, she's not taking it well. I don't know how to explain this in a good way. I haven't even told her we can only visit from outside."

"Outside?"

"We can go as far as the grounds, not into the sanitarium. She can stand by her window while we wave to her from the lawn," Dina said. "No hugs. When she starts to heal, she can get fresh air in the sun, though we still won't be allowed to get close."

"It's such a cold way to see a child. Why can't she rest at home?"

"That's exactly what she asked. She's too contagious. Do you understand what that means?"

"For God's sake, of course I know what it means. You can catch tuberculosis from her."

"It's not so simple. Anyone who comes here and anyone we're with can catch TB. If she stays home, we have to hide her so the neighbors won't find out. We'd have to make up a story. Nobody, not even her teacher or classmates can know what she has or our apartment, and all of us, will be quarantined."

Suddenly there was a wail from Rachel who had gotten out of bed again and tiptoed to the kitchen to listen to her mother's conversation.

"Does Grandma know?" Rachel said. "She won't let you send me away."

"Your grandmother knows you need medicine and bed rest. She wants you to recover. I haven't told her about the clinic. Grandpa promised to help make her understand."

"Even with Grandpa on your side, Grandma likes to do whatever she did in the old country. She won't let you send me away."

"I know that if something is different, Grandma says '*feh.*' This time she saw blood on your hankie. She realizes her old remedies won't work as well as the new medicine. It's called Streptomycin and we hope it will be the cure."

"Hope! Mommy, you aren't sure it will work and you're still sending me away!"

"The doctors know what they're doing. We have to trust them. We must do whatever we can. Think the best thoughts, not the worst. It will work!" she said, hanging up the phone.

Rachel began to cry again, then coughed. Her hankie was filled with so many spots of blood she wiped her nose with the sleeve of her pajamas.

"Oh, Rachel," Dina said. "I'm so sorry you heard all this because I'm sure it isn't as bad as it sounds. The place has beautiful grounds with lots of grass and trees."

"I don't care about the grass and trees."

"There will be other children and books and games, like checkers."

"I want to stay home. I'm scared and I'm worried."

"I'll tell you a secret. You don't have to worry because Daddy and I are going to do all the worrying for you," she said, trying to sound persuasive. "All you have to do is rest."

"Why did this happen to me? It's not fair."

"Life's not always fair. We'll get through it together."

"You told Aunt Sarah you'll only visit me from outside." Rachel said, while coughing up some phlegm into her already soaked handkerchief. "That's not together. I'm afraid."

"I understand," Dina said, tossing the hankie in the garbage and giving her daughter a freshly ironed one. "Think about all the new friends you'll have. And lots of nurses will take care of you. I'm sure there will be many quiet activities, like arts and crafts. You love arts and crafts. If you stay here, you'll be all alone in your room with nothing to do except read. When you go to the clinic, it will be harder for me and for Daddy, yet better for you."

"That's not true! You're not getting shots. You're not away from Daddy. You can visit Grandma and Grandpa and Leah. It won't be harder for you."

Rachel started to cry, then cough again. She twisted her old pink baby blanket that had faded to beige over the past nine years. Her finger slipped through one of its many holes as she continued to whimper. It took some time for her to calm down enough to stop sobbing.

"Rachel, I don't think you realize how serious this is. You need the medicine. Try to sleep a little. Then we can pack a small bag with some of your favorite things. Later today, Daddy will be home and we'll take you to the doctor."

"Can I have a hug before I rest?"

"I can't hug you." Dina said, as she tried to hide another round of tears trickling down her cheeks. "I think I can rub your back while you face the other way."

Rachel was too overwhelmed by another long coughing fit to be able to respond. She shuffled to her room and sat on her bed as her mother combed her tangled blonde hair. She was too exhausted to sit up for long so she lay down and let her mother cover her with the new quilt Grandma had made.

Once her mother left the room, Rachel got up, put on her shoes in slow motion, then threw her blue robe over her PJ's. Despite feeling lethargic, she stood by the door until the sound of her mother's footsteps disappeared. First, she paced in circles trying to decide what to do. With a burst of energy, she grabbed her favorite stuffed dog, snuck out of the apartment and walked around the block to Leah's house. It was early afternoon and despite the bright sun, her robe was not enough protection from the cold winter air. She hugged herself, continuing to move slowly, aware that if she walked at a normal pace, she would start to cough again.

The two flights of steps were her next problem, even though the landlord had covered them with thick burgundy carpet before he raised the rent. Climbing took away her breath so she sat down and pulled herself up with her arms, resting in between. By the time she finished trudging to the landing near Leah's apartment, she had to rest again. A few minutes later, she tried the door handle. No luck. Usually, the front door was unlocked. With Grandma wandering off sometimes, visitors now needed to ring the bell. She couldn't sneak in.

Then she spotted a nearby flowerpot. A shiny key was sticking out of the soil near the plastic plant. Maybe it was there so that if Grandma wandered out and closed the door, she could get back inside. Rachel used the key, replaced it in the pot and faced another hurdle, a new gate that was also locked. She threw her stuffed dog into the apartment and climbed up, practically falling over. That's when she started to cough, consuming what felt like her last bit of energy. Inside, everything was quiet except for the television that was blasting in the living room where Grandma sat. It must have drowned out Rachel's sounds. Rachel didn't see Aunt Sarah, or Grandpa, so she dragged her feet into Leah's room. Her cousin was huddled at her desk doing homework, practicing penmanship in a new notebook.

"Rachel," Leah said. "What are you doing here? What's the matter? You don't look so good. Why are you wearing your PJs?"

"Shh," Rachel said, with her index finger covering her lips. "Mommy and Daddy want to send me away. They want me to go to a clinic to live. All alone. Well, not all alone," she said, then started to cry. "I'll be with other children, but they'll also be sick. And I'll have to get shots. I won't go."

"Rachel, a shot doesn't hurt for long. It's quick and not so bad. If it will stop your coughing, of course you should go."

"That's easy for you to say. You won't be separated from everyone. You'll still be going to school."

"Well, what do you want to do?"

"I want to hide in your special place, the one you told me about. Where you keep your silver dollars."

Leah chewed on her pencil's eraser and stared at her cousin, then rested the pencil down on her notebook.

"Okay," she said, "it's not very big so you won't be able to lie down and sleep. And there's no place to pee. Besides, if you cough, everyone will hear you."

"Can I sit? I don't cough as much if I sit."

"There's enough room to sit. When I close the door, it will get creepy dark and there's a big hole in the back of the floor. You have to be careful not to fall through. I don't think this is such a good idea."

"You don't like it because it's my idea. You always decide what we do. This time I'm deciding and I want to hide. I'm not going to any stupid clinic."

"Okay, okay. I'll show you the closet. I've never stayed there for more than a few minutes. Even if I sneak food to you, this won't work for long."

"We can come up with another plan while I'm hiding there. It's the best place for right now."

"I have to jiggle the knob for the door to unlock. It opens easily from inside in case you want to come out."

"I'm not coming out so fast. Not until I have another plan."

"Everyone will ask me where you are. What should I tell them?"

"Tell them you don't know."

"That's a lie. Sometimes I keep quiet and sometimes I don't tell all the truth, but I never lie."

"So, keep quiet. Or make up something. Just promise me you won't tell anyone where I am."

"I promise. I still think you're making a mistake. Doctors are smart and helpful, better than Grandma's old-fashioned cures. Someday, I'm going to be a doctor even though Mommy says I have to be a teacher. Daddy says I can be whatever I want to be and I want to help people with lung diseases. They do things the American way. Don't you want to be a real American and go to the doctor?"

"That's stupid. I was born here. I'm already an American. I need to hide. I'm going to pee first and then you can take me to the closet."

Together they tiptoed to the kitchen. Leah looked in the pantry for a box of cookies to give to her cousin. Then she jiggled the knob of the closet door. Rachel slithered in and Leah shut the hiding place. She looked around one more time. All the adults were busy in different rooms. She walked back to her desk to continue practicing her penmanship, determined to get another A so her father would give her another silver dollar.

The only give-away that she was nervous was the tap, tap tapping of her bare foot on the floor as she tried to sit still. It was no use. She had to check on her cousin so she crept to the kitchen and leaned her ear against the closet door.

"Shh, Rachel. I can hear my silver dollars clinking together. You can count them later. Right now, you have to be quiet," Leah said.

"Who are you talking to?" Leah's mother yelled from her bedroom.

"Nobody. I was just getting a cookie," she hollered before returning to her homework.

Less than fifteen minutes later, Grandma stormed into Leah's room.

"Vere is she? Vat did you do vit your cousin?" she said, not sounding at all confused.

Leah tried keeping quiet. Grandma wouldn't stop asking.

"Don't make believe you don't hear me. Vere is your cousin? You always like to hide. Vere did you put her?"

Again, Leah kept silent. Grandma came closer, their noses almost touching. She looked angrier than when Leah had tried to get a polio shot without permission last year. Keeping her promise to Rachel was not going to be easy.

Grandma put her gnarled fingers on Leah's shoulders and shook her. She shook her so forcefully Leah's head flopped back and forth.

"You tell me now. Vere is your cousin," she said, shaking Leah even harder, her voice getting louder, spilling out her fear and anger.

"Dina vent to tuck her in bed. She vasn't in her room. I know you know vere she is. Tell me now!"

Leah's head kept rocking forward and back. Her chin hit her scrawny chest then her head was thrown in reverse. Grandma's strength was surprisingly powerful. Leah didn't believe her head would actually fall off though it sure felt like it would. She started to scream.

Grandma pushed Leah's shoulders harder as Sarah came out of her room and begged her to stop. Grandpa was there too, pulling Grandma's hands off of Leah. They could hear the neighbor downstairs banging on her ceiling with her broom.

"Okay," Leah said, sort of glad Grandma was forcing her to reveal where Rachel was hiding.

She wanted her cousin to get the shots and be saved. She even promised herself that if Rachel were saved, she would not smoke cigarettes like her father always did.

"Stop shaking me," she shouted while gulping air. "She's in the closet."

Grandma moved back and caught her breath.

"Vich closet?"

"The secret one in the kitchen. I'll show you."

Leah took her grandmother's hand and marched to the kitchen. One jiggle and the door flung open. Grandma grabbed Rachel who was crying and coughing quietly into her stained handkerchief.

"Your parents are so vorried. It's too late to go to the clinic today. Tomorrow you vill go," Grandma said. "Tomorrow no more hiding."

"You promised," Rachel whined to her cousin as she was pulled toward the stairs. "Tomorrow I'll be in the clinic and it's all your fault."

19. A Long Week

Momism: The past matters.

"You seem a little flustered when you're in the same room with Roberto," Kevin said. "Anything I should know?"

"No. Nothing. Except, he's in the way. We're opening in a few days and have so much to accomplish. His psychobabble is distracting."

"I was under the impression you liked it. The aura business and bringing out your shining light made you smile when he arrived."

"That was for the first two days. It's gotten annoying. He won't go to a museum or a show or anything without Francesca and I need her with me. He has no reason to be here other than being with his wife."

"We like to be together. Why does it bother you that he feels the same way about being with his wife?" Kevin said, tilting his head and smiling before he put on one of his many white shirts he wears to the office.

"Can we drop it? Talk about something more relevant? Maybe you can stop by the store later and help unpack some of the boxes Francesca sent from Italy."

"Sounds like a good activity for Roberto," Kevin said, with that same teasing grin. "I'm doing surgery today and won't be free until tonight."

"Roberto it is," I said, pursing my lips, trying not to appear rattled. "He and Francesca are meeting me at the boutique at 11:00. I have an hour there on my own."

When I arrived at the shop, I was surprised to see John waiting outside. Maybe he had some important information to share, though it was odd that he didn't call first.

"Hello, Susan," he said. "I came to see how the store is coming along. Ready for the opening?"

"Almost," I said, noticing he was wearing a pressed ice-blue shirt that brought out the gorgeous color of his eyes again. Blue was definitely his color. His jeans were tight. A navy sweater was thrown over his shoulders with the sleeves tied in front, creating a casual appearance that was obviously well planned. He'd even abandoned his socks and substituted tan loafers for his sneakers.

"You're looking pretty spiffy," I said. "Going somewhere special?"

"Here. That's special. Where's your team?"

"Francesca?" I said, just as a cab pulled up. She was an hour early. I watched her get out of the car, all legs in her short, low-cut dress and high heels. I noticed John watching, too. Roberto was with her. Before I could welcome them, John stepped in front of me and took the lead.

"Hello Francesca," he said, in his best voice-over tone while towering over her, bending a little to take her hand, the one with the wide gold wedding band. At least he didn't kiss it. "So nice to see you again."

"*Piacere*, pleased to see you," she said, turning on her charm. Their eyes locked, followed by simultaneous smiles before John turned toward her husband who was wearing a matching wide gold wedding band I hadn't noticed before. Maybe Roberto wore it only when he was with his wife.

John acknowledged him with a nod, nothing more, then turned back to Francesca, oozing sexual tension, or maybe my overactive imagination was kicking in. I wondered if Sean's future father-in-law was a philanderer? I wasn't sure if I would ignore it or share my suspicion with my son.

You're in no position to take the moral highroad, my mother said. *Besides, all he did was get cleaned up.*

John took the lead again.

"I trust you slept well," he said to Francesca.

I rolled my eyes, letting him know I thought it was a stupid statement.

"What?" he said, in his booming voice, encouraging everyone to look my way. I clammed up, dug inside my bag of hope for my keys and opened the store.

Once inside, the four of us walked around piles of cardboard boxes as if we had been part of a scheduled meeting. I decided to take advantage of having extra hands and asked everyone to start opening the cartons. Roberto hovered near me, way too close. Francesca, followed by John, took two boxes to the front of the shop and began taking out dresses, blouses and slacks to hang along the crisp white walls. Steaming would come later.

"Roberto, what are you waiting for? I bet your wife can use some help," I said, wondering why his shirt was unbuttoned to the middle of his chest letting his gray and black hairs escape. Where did he think he was?

"Ah," he said, "she is content to work with John. He is your manager, no?"

"No. John is the father of my son's girlfriend. I'm not sure why he came here." It sounded critical so I added, "Though he's welcome, of course. He's a detective helping me figure out what happened to the skeleton."

"And he has a wife?" Roberto said, as if it were a normal question.

"Yes."

"Is she beautiful?"

"We haven't met," I said, moving to the back to grab a bottle of water from the mini refrigerator. Roberto followed.

"She'll come to opening night. All I know is that her name is Nancy and she's a nurse."

"Ah," he said, standing way too close. I moved toward the orange couch. He trailed, still at my elbow, reminding me of my Golden Retriever.

"I shall call her Nurse Nancy," he said.

"Of course. I know you like to give women nicknames," I said, spilling water on the couch while pushing him away.

Instead of being offended, he pulled out one of the handkerchiefs he carries and mopped up my mess. Why was I always spilling things whenever I was near this man?

"How about helping your wife with the boxes?" I said, wanting my space.

"I am content to watch you. The store is like a light, shining on your inner beauty."

"Enough, Roberto. Stop talking like that. It's silly."

"Silly? It was good in Florence, no?"

"Everything was different in Florence. And stop saying content. It's like when we spoke at the hotel, telling me that with the right attitude, most experiences are able to be happy, happy. It wasn't my real life. Here, in New York, we must be real."

"I do not know what that means," he said. "It was real when you invited me to your room, no?"

"Shh," I said. "Nobody should hear us. It's a secret. Nobody is to know about my mistake. Besides, nothing happened. Remember?"

"I remember everything, *Susanna*. I saw that you are beautiful. That was not a mistake."

"Your wife is beautiful. Leave me alone. You make me nervous. Kevin will notice."

"I want to make you really happy, happy."

"In a few more days you'll go back to Italy. Try to control yourself until you leave. That will make me happy, happy."

By then, John and Francesca had finished hanging up most of the inventory. It was a helpful first try that I could reorganize later. Arranging the display cases in the center of the store was a bigger challenge. It was important to find a balance, not too much merchandise to seem cluttered and not too little to waste space. John was more adept at placing the jewelry than I would have imagined. I really didn't know this man at all. Was something else about to erupt? I was starting to dislike surprises.

"John, do you have any news you want to share?" I asked, hoping for information on the skeleton.

"Nope."

"Just nope?"

"Just nope," he said with his half-grunt laugh. "Place looks great. Don't mind hanging around. Not fishing today."

"Not for fish," I said.

"Something wrong with my being here? Glad to help."

Before I could continue the banter, Roberto shifted too close to me again. At least that's how it felt.

"It's one o'clock. How about we all go to lunch," I said, not really wanting to sit at a table with everyone, yet not wanting to stay in the store with them. "There's a simple Italian place not too far from here. I can use a cappuccino."

Before I could retrieve my handbag and keys from the back office, a tall, young woman appeared at the door. She had gorgeous blue eyes and a generous body that fit with her broad shoulders. Her wide smile lit up her face in a way that made me think of Roberto's phrase about inner beauty. She waved. John waved back then motioned for her to come on in.

20. December, 1954

"Is Rachel here?" Dina shouted as she burst into Sarah's kitchen. "Please, dear God, let her be in your apartment."

"She's not here," Sarah said, putting down her dishtowel and pushing her blonde curls back from her face. "Why do you think she's here?"

"Last night, when Mama brought Rachel home, we put her right to bed. She was furious at Leah and kept mumbling about a secret plan. This morning her bed was empty."

"Calm down," Sarah said, as if she were talking to a child.

"Where is she? She must go to the clinic. Today! She must!!" Dina shouted as she collapsed into a wooden kitchen chair with her head in her hands.

"She's probably hiding in your apartment. I'll go with you. We can look together."

"Stop patronizing me. Don't you think I already searched the place? Ask your daughter. She's in charge of mischief in this family."

"Dina, you know Leah's in school. You can't blame her this time."

"Maybe Rachel went back into the closet. She said her necklace fell off in the hiding place with the silver dollars. Mama yanked her out so fast she didn't have a chance to look for it. Nobody paid attention to her yelling because we wanted to get her out of here. I bet she snuck back after everyone fell asleep."

"We would have heard her."

"Oh no. She's good at moving around silently. And the closet is in the kitchen, nowhere near your bedroom."

"She can't be in the closet. We nailed it shut last night," Sarah said. "A painter is coming later to plaster the wall. If she came here, she couldn't get in."

"Then, where is she? Dina demanded, reaching into her handbag for a cigarette. Her hand shook so violently she could hardly light up her Lucky Strike."

"I don't know. Maybe Mama knows where she is."

The two sisters walked to the front bedroom. Mama wasn't there. Nor was she in the living room in her favorite overstuffed brocade chair, the one with the carved wooden legs placed in front of the TV.

"She's gone again," Dina said, caving in like a balloon losing its air. "They're both missing! They must have gone somewhere together."

"No," Dina snapped sharply. "I know Mama was against the shot at first. After Rachel started to cough up blood, she agreed to allow the medicine."

"If Mama wandered away, she's in one of her confused moments."

"What does that mean for my daughter?"

"It means Mama could take her anywhere. I think Rachel would join her just to get away."

"My daughter has more sense than that. Why do you have to be so critical? It's insulting."

"I'm not being critical. I know your daughter is smart. Why do we have to argue? Why do we have to discuss everything?"

Sometimes, Sarah felt her family was a burden. She wondered what it would be like to live further apart, not to be involved with one another on a daily basis?

"We have to call the police," Dina said, pulling some strands of her new bouffant short hairdo held in place with an excessive amount of hairspray.

"If the police find Mama and try to approach her, she'll be so frightened she'll run from them. Anyway, it's probably too soon. They won't search if someone has been missing just for a few hours," Sarah said.

"I don't care how scared they make her feel," Dina said as she dialed the police. "We need to find them. RACHEL'S IN DANGER," she said, enunciating each word as if her sister were an idiot. "If she doesn't get Streptomycin soon, she'll get worse."

Dina stubbed out her cigarette, then reached for another. Sarah watched as Dina lit up again, her hands trembling.

"I want to report a missing person," she said between deep drags of smoke. "Two people, actually. My mother and my daughter."

Dina provided basic information before hanging up. Once again, she crushed the half-smoked cigarette then put her head back in her hands.

"The police were not so concerned about Mama because she hasn't been gone for more than a few hours. When they heard Rachel was almost ten, they said they're sending someone over."

When the police arrived, they questioned both Dina and Sarah. Fortunately, the details they shared supported each other.

"Will you put out an alarm?" Dina said.

"I'm sorry, ma'am. We need to check every possibility before we go that route," the cop said. "First, we need to open the closet you mentioned."

"And if you don't find them, what happens next?"

"We search the area and send out a missing person's bulletin. I don't want to scare you, but I noticed a mezuzah outside your door. There has been some anti-Semitic graffiti painted on the synagogue on the corner of this street. It might be a hate-related situation. Has anyone sent you nasty messages or accosted your family in any way?"

"Oh my God! I feel dizzy," Dina said, throwing the remains of her latest cigarette into the kitchen sink, then digging in her purse for another one. "No. Nobody hates us."

"I'll need a description of both parties, ma'am. Photos too. Birth dates. Approximate weight for each one. When were they last seen?"

Dina lit her cigarette, inhaled deeply, then faced the officer with what seemed like a new resolve to get to work.

"My daughter is beautiful. She has blonde hair and blue eyes like my sister over there," Dina said, pointing to Sarah. "And she's smart. I don't believe she's lost. And I don't think something bad, God forbid, happened to her. This is a safe place for people to live. I think she ran away on purpose. She won't want you to find her because she's sick, coughing all the time. You might hear her if she's hiding."

"Do you recall what she was wearing, ma'am?"

"I have no clue. She slid away in the night so maybe she's in her pajamas. If not, most of her dresses are some shade of blue, her favorite color. Her jacket is navy."

"Can you tell us anything else that might be helpful?"

"Well, she likes to eat, especially cakes and sweets. Maybe she'll try to get something from the local bakery if she brought her allowance with her. I don't know how much was planned and how much was spontaneous."

Another cop arrived carrying a crow bar and hammer. He plied off the wood that Solly had nailed across the closet door. Both officers looked in. One stepped inside and used his flashlight to look through the hole down below.

"Nothing's there. I see a whole lot of dust," he said, "and it smells like there was a fire. You can close it up."

"We did have a fire in our kitchen, though that was a while ago."

After the police left, Dina and Sarah decided to scour the neighborhood on their own. Dina moved toward her home around the corner. Sarah strode in the other direction. None of the shopkeepers had seen an older woman or child, alone or together.

When Leah's grandfather brought her home from school, the two of them went into the kitchen to make a glass of hot tea and a hot chocolate.

"*Vere's* Rachel?" he said softly. "Did you hide her again? She's gone and your aunt and mother are *vorried.*"

"I didn't hide her, Grandpa."

"My *shayna maidel* is gone, too. She probably took Rachel for a *valk*. If you know, you'll tell us. No more secrets. It's too important to find *dem.*"

"I don't know anything," Leah said, starting to cry. "I hope nothing terrible happened. Will Grandma know how to get home this time?"

"*Vee* all hope nothing bad happened," Grandpa said. "*Tink* the best and *dey vill* be here soon."

"I bet Rachel went back into the closet. I taught her how to jiggle the door open and she liked my silver dollars."

"Your daddy sealed the closet last night, after you *vent* to bed."

"Open it up," she begged. "Please, let me get my silver dollars."

"The police *vere* here *vile* you *vere* in school. They opened the door and looked for Rachel and Grandma. *Dey vere* not *dere* so they nailed the door shut again. Vee are not allowed to touch it anymore."

Grandpa got up to bring some Oreo cookies to the kitchen table.

"Did they find my silver dollars?"

"No. You'll get new *vones*," he said, pouring the milk into Leah's special cup to cool down her chocolate drink. "*Dat* space is a death trap."

"I like having it as a secret place. Why is it here?"

"You mean the closet? *Dis* whole building used to be owned by *von* rich family. Most likely *dat's* how *dey* threw their laundry down to the ground floor."

"I want to open it just one more time. Once more. Please," Leah said.

"*Dat's vat* the police did. They tore it open and looked down with *dere* flashlights. *Dey* found *noting*."

"Why are you so calm, Grandpa? Why aren't you crying and yelling like Mommy and Aunt Dina?"

"I believe *dey vill* come back soon. I believe *noting* bad happened."

Leah took a deep breath, then dipped her cookie into her drink. Together they sat quietly.

"Wait a minute. Maybe they're both downstairs visiting the neighbors," Leah said, as Aunt Dina and Sarah returned and joined them at the table.

"Why would they be there?" Dina said. "Sarah told me the wife is only nice when she's with her husband. They're still upset at the smell from your fire. And their six kids are wild. Rachel is too weak to put up with them."

"The neighbors have been very worried about Mama and offered to help," Sarah said. "We have to try everything."

Just then, the doorbell rang. It was Rachel and her grandmother.

21. A Difficult Encounter

Momism: Don't judge a book by its cover.

The girl came in and hugged John before they both walked over to me. I tried not to act startled when he introduced his daughter, annoyed that Sean allowed us to meet without warning me. Maybe my son didn't know. Maybe it was all John's idea.

Before I had a chance to respond, John ushered Sophie over to Roberto and Francesca. Now, all conversation would be part of a group with no opportunity to have a private chat.

I looked at this woman who might become my daughter-in-law. She had beautiful blonde hair that cascaded over her shoulders. Her orange and blue patterned skirt hung on her ample body like an afterthought, not shabby, not fashionable. Of course, I noticed, then pushed away the fact that it bothered me, attempting to leave my superficial values about image back at the ad agency where they belonged.

I tried to focus on her welcoming smile, her pretty face that my son would look at every day if they married, hoping we could find something in common. I watched Roberto take her hand, heard him say *piacere,* acting as if she were the most gorgeous, sexy woman. Sophie beamed, seeming to enjoy the attention.

After all the formalities were covered, she turned to me. For the sake of my son, I knew I had to become a better person, at least in this situation. I plunged in, determined to be friendly. We shook hands, my freshly manicured red nails contrasted with her all-natural look.

"Hello, Mrs. Kendall," she said, folding and unfolding her hands. "Sean has told me so many lovely things about you. I'm glad we're finally connecting."

I laughed to myself, wanting to say *piacere,* to cover everything with one word and move on. Then I turned serious. This was an important moment. I wished Kevin were here to help me or at least stand by my side and charm her in his diplomatic way.

"Please, call me Susan. Sorry for the mess in here," I said swinging my arm around to encompass the total environment that wasn't so messy. "We're opening in two days and we'll have all the garments steamed and customer-ready by then."

"I'm sure. Sean says you're the most efficient person he knows," she said, looking down at her hands the way her father had done during our meetings at Panera. "My dad insisted I come by today and get it over with, our initial contact, that is, if you know what I mean."

I did know what she meant. She sounded so nervous and insecure. At least she wasn't cracking her knuckles like her dad. At this point, John put his arm around his daughter. I wasn't sure how much Francesca and Roberto understood our conversation, though they remained close by and nodded their heads at the right moments.

You said you want to become a better person, my mother said. *Now's the time to help the girl out.*

Sophie was very tall, as tall as John had mentioned. I had to look up to talk to her or I'd be staring at her chest and neck.

"Welcome to my new world," I said, then felt silly, calling my shop a whole world. I sensed my face flush with that tell-all rash. Now, everyone knew I was nervous. Where was Sean when I needed him?

We all looked at each other, remaining silent. I'd interviewed many young people while working at the ad agency. Certainly, I could move this awkward moment into something pleasant, if not substantial. John was smiling, so perhaps everything was okay.

"Come, let me give you a tour. I rented two stores and knocked down a wall to combine them."

"Yes," she said. "I heard there was a skeleton inside that wall. It must have been quite a surprise."

"Can't get away from it, no matter how I try."

"Oh, I'm sorry. I shouldn't have brought it up. Can we change the subject? I see you like neutral colors," she said, looking around.

Sophie moved along the wall, touching black, navy and gray trousers and skirts, passing by the white, beige and cream tops, looking at labels, sizes and price tags. When she saw the $800 cost of a silk blouse, she blinked and her mouth opened. As I watched Sophie regain control over her shock, I felt a little uncomfortable, even though the price was perfectly normal for my clientele, a bargain compared to Valentino or Gucci.

"How come you only carry up to size six? All your customers must be pixies. I wear size 12 and Mom is a 14," she said. "I guess we can never buy here, not that we could afford to."

"We keep the larger sizes in back."

"Why?"

"Fewer garments provide more space to display the clothes as if they're pieces of art. And don't worry about the cost. You'll always get a hefty, I mean, substantial discount if you want anything."

"That's very generous, but I would never take advantage of you. Besides, I like bright colors. They make me happy," she said, looking at me in my standard black slacks and white silk blouse.

Another silence engulfed us. They were getting more difficult to ignore.

"Enough about the store," I said. "Tell me about your studies. Is the Icahn School of Medicine at Mt. Sinai as special as Sean claims?"

I knew I was ridiculous stating the complete name of the school we were already familiar with, had even donated to. I was proud my boy was studying medicine at such a top place. Talking about it was my way to shift the conversation.

"Is that where you two met?"

"Yes," Sophie said. "In the cafeteria, last year. It turned out we had two classes together. Sean's so smart. And supportive. I have to plug along, reading and rereading our assignments. I don't stop until all the information is internalized. It's such a responsibility to be a doctor. I can't fathom not remembering something we've been taught, so once I've mastered a lesson, I reread it just to be sure I've got it."

"At least Sean's a quick study."

"Oh no," Sophie said. "He gets the big picture right away, then works really hard to retain all the details. It's one of the things we have in common—studying long hours together."

I wondered how this girl thinks she knows my son better than I do. It's only their second year in medical school. Not enough togetherness compared to my time as his mother.

"Are you sure you're talking about my Sean? He's never had to grind away to get good grades. He always laughed off my demands to do homework."

"Don't be fooled by his attitude," Sophie said. "He labors at his assignments."

I pursed my lips. Who was this girl to tell me about my child! Sophie broke out in a sweat I could see forming on her forehead. Roberto handed her a handkerchief. It was time to end this meeting.

John, who was busy talking to Francesca about God knows what, would be no help. Turns out Roberto saved me. I watched him take Sophie's hand.

"You have an aura about you," he said with his Italian accent. "The colorful skirt you are wearing brings out your inner light."

Sophie beamed at him, muttering something about seeing all of us again real soon. Then Roberto walked her out the door so she could return to school. It was the first time I was truly grateful for his psychobabble.

22. *Susanna's* Opens

Momism: Don't share everything.

Kevin and Roberto sat in the small, gray leather armchairs adorned with orange pillows near the back of the shop. It was a place for husbands or friends to rest and enjoy a cappuccino from our new machine. It made me nervous to see them together. I know Roberto perceives nothing wrong with our flirtation. Okay, it was more than a flirtation. I doubt he'll say anything about us, but there's no guarantee. I grabbed another glass of prosecco, put on my everything-is-all-right face and joined them.

"I trust you two are behaving yourselves," I said, standing near the orange couch that made the space appear as welcoming as a living room in someone's home.

"See the lights in the ceiling and how they reflect the radiance the boutique is offering," Kevin said with an enormous smile, then added, "in addition to Francesca's numerous designs."

What kind of nonsense was my husband pulling, trying to match Roberto's psychobabble? My nerves were already on edge without the sarcastic comments. Maybe my Italian rogue wouldn't realize he was the brunt of Kevin's supposed humor.

Be happy Kevin is keeping Roberto away from the customers, Mom said.

I glimpsed my reflection in a mirror above the couch. My face was pale and tense. Kevin and Roberto raised their glasses of prosecco in unison as if they were a team. Not a good sign.

I turned back to the clothes I had rearranged at least three times. Jackets and skirts were settled on the lower racks against the long wall. There was plenty of space between each piece. Recessed lights under the shelves above illuminated the garments below.

Blouses filled the top sections. Dresses and pants floated in a similar presentation on the other long wall. Maybe I should tweak the arrangement one more time.

Stop, my mother said. *Don't redo what's done.*

"It took me two days to steam the clothes the way I liked them," I said. No one was close enough to hear me.

Of course, I had rearranged the display at the central table for the third time. Our upscale costume jewelry and scarves needed to pop, to pull in a client and entice her to enhance a new outfit with a spontaneous purchase. Satisfied that everything glistened, I was ready. Well, the store was ready. I still needed to project confidence.

While pacing nervously, I was drawn to the front door to greet our friends and family who were already arriving, munching on the hors d'oeuvres passed around by young waitstaff in tuxedos.

At that moment, I saw Leah standing outside, staring at the smaller window. What was she doing here? She wore black, looking even more elegant than the last time she showed up, obviously a woman who spent money on her wardrobe.

The timing was not good. Francesca, in her signature red dress and me, in the gray version, were poised to talk to the press. Fingers crossed they would show up as promised. Double fingers crossed they would concentrate on our fashions rather than the gruesome skeleton. No guarantees there, either. Much as I yearned to talk to Leah, she was a distraction. Then John entered with Sean and Sophie. No wife.

"Nancy can't get off work until later," he said while looking over my shoulder.

"She'll meet us at dinner."

Though he was wearing sneakers, he also wore crisp jeans, a button-down blue shirt and dark blazer. He looked kind of cool. I wasn't surprised he immediately found Francesca.

She acknowledged him with a wink and a wide smile. They had moved close enough to the back of the boutique for Roberto to see them together. He nodded acknowledgement, then ignored them. Didn't Europeans get jealous? Maybe it was all just my overactive imagination projecting a connection that didn't exist. Everyone seemed to be happy, happy.

Sophie appeared more relaxed with Sean's arm around her. They stood in front of me, not quite equal in height. Like last time, she wore bright colors in a geometric pattern. She was munching on a canapé. I looked at her and was glad I controlled my head from moving back and forth in a silent "no, don't eat that. It's fattening."

"Love your windows, Mom. Everything is as elegant as you are," Sean said, continuing to hold onto Sophie.

"Are you flattering me?"

"Of course. But it's true. Nothing overdone. Nothing too understated to be boring. Just right for your target audience."

Ever the charmer, he lowered his arm from Sophie's waist and bent in to give me a peck on the cheek.

"I'm glad you two met," he said, while stepping behind Sophie so she could extend her hand. I didn't want to shake it in case her fingers had leftover crumbs so I gave her a fist bump. She did the same, then rolled her eyes.

I could feel my face flush. It's never the right time for a rash to appear. This was one of the worst times. On top of all the personal chaos, I now worried that other customers who ate canapés would soil the clothes. Serving food was a big mistake.

"Dad's in the back," I said, moving them off so I could concentrate on potential buyers and reporters. I wanted to explain why our clothes were different, to let the media know that whether my labels said size zero, two, four and up, each piece would have an extra inch or two to fit comfortably around wider hips and fuller breasts.

I also wanted to provide details about our smallest window, the one that still captured Leah's attention. It had given us so much creative trouble. Now it held child-size hangers and special outfits thanks to Jennifer. I believed her suggested display was a brilliant way to acknowledge the skeleton in a positive way. Since we didn't know if the bones belonged to a boy or girl, we opted to create an outfit for each. We planned to auction off the clothes at a later date, then give the proceeds to charity. That would be my response to questions about the tragedy we inadvertently uncovered—doing something good.

Since Leah seemed fascinated, I went outside to talk to her. Instead of sharing enthusiasm about the display, she lashed into me.

"This is awful," she said, softly. "The skeleton is a girl. One girl. You shouldn't have two outfits."

"Why didn't you tell me the first time you came here? You have no idea how hard it was to figure out what to do."

Leah frowned. How dare she come here and complain! I didn't even know if this woman was authentic, if she knew what had happened or was some nut. I decided to give her the benefit of doubt until I heard her story.

"My favorite part of the presentation is the burgundy dress," I said, feeling uncomfortable to be speaking about fashion, yet unable to stop. "It's as simple as the adult clothing with hidden pockets in the A-line skirt. The top features matching sequins just above the waist and a conservative jewel neckline so a preteen can wear a necklace or one of the lace collars we're selling separately. The dress is paired with Gucci Matilda Ballet Flats and a Sylvie Bow."

Leah glared at me. "It's not the way she was. And no boy in our neighborhood would ever dress like this."

I turned to the boy's version—a burgundy sweater draped over the hanger sporting a light blue, button-down shirt, slim tan pants and Gucci Jordaan leather loafers priced a tad over $400. Maybe I should have picked up a pair of kids' jeans and gone downtown to Flight Club to select Air Jordan sneakers.

"Leah, I have no idea what happened or who this happened to. I did the best I could with no information. We're trying to create something positive. Read the plaque at the base of the display."

These outfits are dedicated to
the innocent child who lost his or her life
in this building many years ago.
Bids for the purchase will be accepted all week.
Proceeds will be donated to the
Find The Children charity.

"You're exploiting a tragedy to get good publicity. I find this offensive," Leah said. Then to my horror, she entered the store.

I followed, watching her glide around the shop, touch the display cabinet and some skirts on a bottom rack. I saw her raise her eyes to the ceiling, seeming to search for something. I wanted to grab her hand and bring her to my back office to hear all the facts about the skeleton. Unfortunately, one cannot always do what one wants, no matter how searing the desire. I needed to work the room and chat up the press—without Leah, without all the other distractions that were crashing down on me.

By now, John had noticed her and left Francesca to be by Leah's side. After a gentle hello, he tried to engage her in conversation. I moved next to them.

"Have you gone to the police," he asked. "How can we tell you really know what happened?"

"Tomorrow," she said to both of us, fingering the Star of David that hung round her neck. "I'll be back in the morning."

"It's a date," I said.

Then she left, seeming to slither out the door just as a reporter from *New York* magazine came in.

23. The Big Dinner

Momism: Every marriage is different.

"Sean, you take Sophie and her parents to the restaurant in one taxi. We'll take Francesca and Roberto in another," I said, glad the party was over. "It's called Uva, over on Second Avenue between 77th and 78th."

"We're going to need three cabs," Sean said, taking charge. "Dad can bring Francesca and Roberto."

"What about me?" I said, wondering how I was going to get through this celebratory dinner.

"You go with John and Nancy. It'll give you a chance to chat. Sophie and I and Jennifer will meet you over there."

I had to accept his request, not start a family spat in front of everyone. I looked at Nancy. Her eyes were kind, belonging to a person anyone would appreciate to have as a nurse. But—with me there's always a but—her salt and pepper hair would benefit from a brown rinse. Kevin could remove the extra skin on her neck and a little Botox and Juvederm would take years off her appearance, not that it mattered.

Stop trying to remake everyone, Mom said. *Don't tell people how to live, or worse, how to look.*

Mom was right. I always impose my ideals. If I want to be a better person, I have to stop. Maybe being aware of my fault is step one in a 12-step program against being judgmental and having superficial values.

"Nancy, it's nice to finally meet you. John has been so helpful trying to solve the case of the skeleton," I said, nodding toward her husband.

"Nice to meet you, too. John says you've got a great mind. He thinks you should take up detective work on the side."

"I'm afraid sleuthing got pushed to the bottom of my list until the renovations were complete. I needed to concentrate on opening the store. Investigating is next."

We smiled quietly. As we drove, I could hear a horn honk and traffic moving. Inside the cab, silence lingered, while in my mind I continued to redo Nancy. It's hard to change after so many years creating the best images possible at the ad agency. I was determined to do better and tried to bury my critical thoughts. The best I could do was keep my mouth closed and we all know how tough that is for me.

I wondered if Sophie were ambitious. She already climbed above her parents the minute she entered medical school. I hoped she didn't see Sean as a way to improve her social status.

Are you jealous she'll steal your son? Mom said. *It's too late. She already has. That's how it should be.*

Maybe I am a little jealous. My son has so little time for me. Perhaps he really loves her. Maybe they truly love each other. Meanwhile, the awkward stillness was becoming unbearable while Nancy and I smiled again.

"Aren't we lucky Sean and Sophie found each other?" she said, breaking the artificial calm.

By some miracle, there was very little traffic and we arrived at Uva in what seemed like a nano second, saving me from having to answer. I needed time to see just how lucky we all are.

Inside the restaurant, I started to organize the seating, but quickly lost control.

Francesca had already taken a chair against the wall at the end of one of the long sides of the rectangular table. John immediately grabbed the chair next to her. No surprise there. Then came Sophie, seemingly happy to sit by her father with Sean on her other side. Four guests down and six more to arrange counting an empty seat for Jen's husband, Adam, who would join us soon.

"Mom, you're hosting so why don't you sit at the head of the table," Jennifer said, pulling out the end chair near Sean. "Daddy can sit at the other end."

"Lovely," I said, trying to be diplomatic, waving to Kevin as he blew me a kiss.

The minute I was settled, Roberto immediately grabbed the seat to my left. Not what I wanted. I bit my lip to help myself keep quiet. "Let go," I kept muttering to myself. "Let the evening flow."

Jen sat next to Roberto with Adam's empty place to her left. Nancy placed herself to the right of Kevin, facing Francesca.

Once we were all settled, the waiter took our order for drinks and then delivered my preorder of tomato bruschetta and an appetizer of mixed Italian cold meats—mortadella, sopressata, prosciutto and cheeses for everyone to share. What followed was another surprise. Sean stood up and took over again.

"Congratulations, Mom and Francesca," he said, raising his glass of Macallan on the rocks, a taste he acquired from his dad. "Here's to a wonderful new beginning for both of you—in great style, of course."

We all cheered and sipped our beverages. I swear I saw John wink at me before Sean continued.

"Speaking of new beginnings, this is your night," he said, turning his head toward me. "But it's also a special evening Sophie and I probably will remember for our entire lives."

I almost choked on my prosecco.

"This is the first time our four parents are together. A perfect time to let you know that Sophie and I are moving in together as soon as this semester is over. Welcome to our future."

We all cheered again and took more tastes of our drinks. I felt that terrible red rash work its way up from my neck to my cheeks. Everyone applauded while I clutched my glass and beamed my everything-is-all-right smile. Only everything wasn't all right. Roberto was rubbing his leg on mine under the table.

At first, I thought it was an accident. When I didn't react, he rubbed me again, then kept his leg plastered against my calf. I shifted away. He adjusted his chair to be able to reach me, a rather overt move considering everyone surrounding us. I guess he enjoyed the game or a flirtatious moment to let me know he still found me attractive. Yuck.

By now the waiter was taking our orders. For a starter, Roberto selected pasta puttanesca—spaghetti with a slightly spicy sauce that Italians claim is the dish of women you'd find in a bordello. Francesca ordered polenta. I settled on my usual salad, dressing on the side, to be followed by filet of sole and steamed asparagus.

When it was Sophie's turn, she chose spaghetti Bolognese. Not very adventurous.

I suppose she doesn't care that pasta is a carb and carbs make you fat. While I was contemplating Sophie's food preferences, I felt fingers on my thigh. Roberto's fingers, making me sorry I had allowed him to sit next to me.

"Stop it," I said, a little too loud with a fake grin directed at Kevin at the other end of the table.

"Stop what?" Sean said. "Don't you like my toasts?"

"Your toasts are perfect," I said while digging my long, polished red nails deep into the skin of Roberto's hand which was still resting on my left leg. I smiled at Sean as I felt Roberto's skin break. Oops, I didn't mean to be so ruthless. That's not what a good person would do.

"*Ow! Mama mia!*" Roberto yelped, raising his hand then slapping it down on the table just as his pasta arrived. His palm landed in his steaming first dish, causing red sauce, perhaps mixed with a tiny bit of his blood, to splatter all over his part of the table and my face.

He used his other hand to grab yet another damn handkerchief from his pocket to cover his wound. A waiter took away his meal, promising to bring a fresh cloth and new portion of pasta. As I wiped my face with a napkin, I noticed John wink at Francesca, perhaps to reassure her that these things happen. We all knew they don't.

Then Kevin winked at me. I was beginning to think the men at the table had developed twitches. For sure, Roberto would not wink at me or touch my thigh, or anyone else's thigh as long as he remained in New York. His discomfort, though well-earned, didn't please me. Instead, I felt badly for Francesca—until I saw her flash a giant smile at John.

I poked a piece of salad with my fork and tried to concentrate on chewing. It was impossible to think about fresh tomatoes or leaves of basil. All that repeated in my head were the words Roberto had told me in Italy.

"Francesca and I have an ideal marriage. She never questions anything I tell her. My heart is pure. That's what counts."

I was grateful he and his pure heart and his ideal marriage were all going back to Italy.

Let it go, Mom said. *This is their life, not yours. Every marriage is different. You are not on this earth to judge.*

Okay, I can do that. I can even join the fun and wink at everyone. The problem is, when I try to wink, I end up squishing up one side of my face as if a bug were in my eye.

Kevin and Nancy were immersed in an intense discussion: one plastic surgeon and one nurse engaged in what I assumed was shoptalk. I hoped she wouldn't criticize my husband for choosing cosmetic surgery that helped pay for this extravagant meal. Maybe they would dance around disagreements and compare the quality of local hospitals and medical insurance. Either way, it seemed they were enjoying one another.

Sophie and Sean had their heads bent together, busy tasting each other's entrees. They looked happy, happy. I wished I could hear what they were whispering and I wished I had sat next to Kevin. Adam had finally arrived and was keeping Jennifer busy.

The pleasant buzz was suddenly broken when Francesca and Roberto started speaking rapidly in

Italian. Since they were on opposite ends of the table, they had to raise their voices and I was sure the entire restaurant could hear them, though nobody understood a word. Then John got up and switched seats with Roberto.

"That Leah lady could be the missing link to your mystery," he said, controlling his booming voice and leaning into me. "I should sit in on your meeting tomorrow."

Thinking about the woman who claimed to once live above the store took me out of the social interactions at the table. Big relief. And I was glad she was going to talk to me before going to the police.

"I want to check her out first. Maybe she won't open up in front of two of us."

24. Susan and Leah

Momism: You're never too old to find a new friend.

Though I was an hour early, Leah was already waiting outside when I arrived. I was relieved to see she exuded a calm and positive demeanor. Once again, her outfit radiated a quiet elegance. Her navy skirt fell just below her knees and her elbows remained covered. The same Star of David she wore last night could be seen on her ice-blue silk shirt that had a round neckline covering her collarbone.

I had checked her out online and she was indeed, a pulmonary specialist at Mt. Sinai Hospital, a professional person. It made me feel hopeful she might be the one to uncover the secrets John and I were searching for. I wondered if we would become friends.

She carried a tote bag with a photo album protruding on top. Sepia-tone images were visible on a page that peeked out of the worn binding. I became edgy thinking she might have pictures of my skeleton when it was a person. The tragic implications overpowered the personal challenge I had created for myself to solve the mystery. My nerves started to seep through my carefully crafted everything-is-okay attitude.

We nodded hello with hesitant smiles before I led her toward my back office. Then she stopped, right where the connecting wall had been.

"Is this where the skeleton was found?" she said.

"Yes. How did you know?"

"It's where the laundry chute ended on the ground floor."

"What laundry chute?"

Instead of answering, she continued to stare at the space, turned her head up to the vaulted ceiling, the modern lights and then the walls lined with hanging clothing.

"The place looks so much bigger than I remember," she said.

"It is bigger. I combined two stores."

"I lived here as a little girl. My grandparents stayed with us in the apartment on the third floor. My cousin, Rachel, lived in the neighborhood and visited all the time."

I watched her take a deep breath. I also took a deep breath, realizing she had lots more to share.

"A large family had the apartment below us. They had six children. Their mother was not my favorite person. Maybe she was too busy with her kids to pay attention to me. Or maybe we weren't religious enough, though we all dressed modestly."

Her comments brought the people who once lived in the building to life.

"Their eldest, Malka, was mean to me. Called me trouble. You can imagine how hurtful that was to a little girl. I didn't have much to do with her four brothers. My friend was Esther, the youngest, who was a year behind me in school."

She stopped speaking for a moment, as if gathering her thoughts.

"I came by last night during your opening party to look at the place and to reflect," she said. "It was too painful to stay. Nothing looks the same."

Leah exhaled slowly, walking around, touching the walls with what seemed like affection.

"Did you know your store used to be a grocery? They prepared the food in the smaller shop. Over there were barrels of pickles," she said, pointing toward a row of skirts. "Above, where your blouses are hanging, were shelves filled with cans of vegetables. Open boxes contained fresh produce—onions and carrots, apples and peaches, depending upon the season. The peaches were so juicy they sometimes dripped on my dress with my first bite. I didn't get in trouble because I was so skinny everyone was happy whenever I ate something."

Decades later and this woman was still thin. *Susanna's* clothes would look terrific on her. I decided to gift her a sample or two.

Leah returned to where the wall had been. I walked alongside, hoping she would tell me who the skeleton was and fearing its relationship to her.

She ambled toward the front door. I followed, glad the store wouldn't open for a while and I could allow her to transport me to another era.

There's more to your boutique than you realized, Mom said.

"The cash register was here, next to the counter where you could see thick sour cream, labneh and cheeses. So many cheeses," she said as we stood near the entrance. "My favorites were Swiss and muenster. Still are."

She turned toward me with the kind of generous smile that says, "I like you."

I could sense that patients at the hospital would have confidence in her.

"Your store smells fresh, like the bouquet of red roses near the front door."

"Thank you," I said. "My husband sent them."

She continued as if she never heard me.

"The grocery also smelled good, but it was a different scent, one that made you hungry. Izzy, that was the name of the grocer, always offered customers something to nibble. He knew what each person liked, and he understood kids. He never gave us the smelly cheeses or the spicy olives."

Leah paused for a moment.

"Try some fresh bread, it's still warm," he'd say, while cutting a thin slice.

I waited, hiding my exasperation that no abbreviated version of her story would be forthcoming.

"I almost taste it on my tongue right now," she said, looking directly at me. She was back in the days of her childhood while my mind was locked in the present. I wished I had some of Kevin's patience.

"Izzy gave us empty wooden cheese boxes," Leah said. "Rachel, and I used them to hold our art supplies, especially the broken crayons that would no longer fit into the crayon cartons."

I was trying not to tap my foot, keeping my mouth shut, waiting and listening until she got to the point of our meeting. At the same time, I was captivated by the world she was describing, a world similar to the one my mom grew up in.

"Sometimes, when my mother was not home, Rachel and I played hide and seek," Leah said. "It was such fun until there was a small fire in our apartment.

Grandma left something on the stove and forgot about it. She was sixty-five, younger than I am now, but she had already become confused."

Alzheimer's or dementia? I didn't ask, wondering if Grandma was the skeleton.

"The fire ruined the kitchen. My parents bought a new Formica table and chairs. They fixed everything except for the smell. The charred odor lasted a long time. I know it reeked in the apartment below us because I used to play down there with Esther."

I assumed that covered the smell of a decaying body. It was a thought too creepy to share, so I kept quiet as we walked to my back office and eased into one of the comfy chairs. I tried not to inflict my opinion, to listen, to start to be a better person.

"What happened that makes you think you know the identity of the skeleton?"

"I'm getting to that," she said. "One of my favorite places to hide was in a closet in the hall near the kitchen. Well, it wasn't really a closet. Later I realized it used to be a laundry chute, the one I mentioned when I first came in. The chute was installed way before we lived here, when the building was for one family and there was no store. There was a similar closet in the lower apartment."

"Did you hide there? If you could throw laundry down, wasn't it an open space with no place to stand?"

"The previous tenants must have put in a floor, but they never completed it. The section closest to the door had wooden boards I could step on. In back there was a hole. Nobody else in my family paid attention to the closet. That's what made it such a good hiding place."

She looked at me with her big dark eyes, an attractive older woman who must have been adorable as a kid. It wasn't just her pretty exterior that was captivating. Somehow, she was drawing me into her life.

"Leah, I see you're wearing a wedding band. What did your husband say about this part of your early family life?" I said, unhappy that my childhood secret and a vision of me with Roberto in Florence both popped into my head.

"I never told him. I haven't told my kids and they are grown with children of their own. When the newspapers carried the story of the bones, it brought everything back and I had to come here."

I shuddered, believing she would identify the person in the wall. Just thinking about it heaved me into her situation like stepping in quicksand. Instead of wanting to get out, I preferred to delve deeper, to know everything.

"The previous residents must have closed off the door to the chute. It was their way of making the area safe," Leah said. "But they didn't do a good job. I could jiggle the knob and slip in. I knew I wasn't allowed to go there, but always had trouble following rules. Still do," she added with her warm smile.

"So, somebody stepped in and fell down," I said. Again, Leah ignored my comment, telling me something else.

"We had a big sadness in our family. My cousin contracted tuberculosis. She was coughing for quite some time. When she coughed up blood, my aunt and uncle finally took her to a doctor."

"When was this? What year?"

"Around 1954."

"That was sixty-three years ago. You've been holding all this inside for most of your life," I said, surprised I wanted to hug her, not daring to move into her space for fear I'd shut her down.

"There was a new antibiotic out by then, Streptomycin, to cure TB," she said. "The antibiotic had to be injected and Rachel was terrified of needles. In addition, she was highly contagious. She could make all of us sick. The doctor was surprised nobody else in her house had caught the disease. He insisted Rachel go to a sanitarium until she got better."

Leah got up and returned to where the wall had been. I followed.

"My cousin came to me crying and told me she wouldn't go. She wouldn't get injections. She begged me to help her. Young as I was, I wished I could cure her. I think that's the moment I decided to become a doctor, a specialist in lung diseases. Of course, that's not the kind of help I gave."

"You hid her, didn't you?"

"Yes, I hid her. I wasn't sure it was the right thing to do. Usually, I was the one who was mischievous, but she was my older cousin and this time, I did as she asked. I showed her my special closet. We jiggled the handle and it opened enough for her to slither inside. I warned her about the hole in the back."

"So, your cousin is our skeleton?"

"When nobody could find Rachel, Grandma came to me. She lived with us. She knew I liked to hide and keep secrets. She knew I always broke rules. 'Vere is Rachel?' my grandma asked. 'Vere did you put her?' Of course, I wouldn't tell. I had promised my cousin I wouldn't say anything."

"What happened next?"

"My grandmother shook me. She shook me so hard my head flopped back and forth. I yelled and cried, but she wouldn't stop. She was short, almost my height. Her eyes were near mine. Grandma didn't seem confused, just angry. 'Vere is she? Vere is she?' She kept yelling in her Russian/Yiddish accent. I was terrified."

"And then what happened?" I said, feeling the horror of the situation, feeling Grandma's fear.

"I told her where Rachel was. Grandma yanked me by my arm and dragged me to the closet. I shook the knob until the door opened and Grandma pushed her way inside, emerging with Rachel."

"Then who's in the wall?" I said. "If it's not Rachel, and not Grandma, why are you telling me about them?"

"Because everything seemed to happen at the same time."

"Everything?"

"First there was the fire. I became frightened of smoke and my father smoked all the time, making me worry his ashes would start another fire. Then Grandma became confused and started to wander, often got lost. I worried she would not come back."

I wanted to fold this woman in my arms like I did to Jennifer when she was little.

"Around this time, swastikas were painted on the outside walls of the local synagogue. I was too scared to go there, even with my grandfather. This was all happening when polio was still a threat and tuberculosis was rampant. And in school we had to practice duck-and-cover under our desks in case there was an atom bomb. Anyone who claims that the old days were easier, doesn't realize what was going on. I became panicky of almost everything."

"Who do you think is in the wall?" I said softly, trying to draw her back to the purpose of our meeting.

"I'm not sure," Leah said.

My heart dropped. Was this a tale that would lead nowhere? I liked Leah and wanted her to be authentic.

"The police found a gold chain and Star of David. Does that help?"

"Almost all the families in our neighborhood were Jewish. Most of the little girls wore a Star of David. It could be anyone. But if it's who I think it is, then it's my fault," she said, tearing up.

"What do you mean, your fault?"

"I mean the person in that wall was there because of me."

"How is that possible?" I didn't dare ask if she pushed someone, but you can bet I thought it. If she did, then the case was a murder—by a child. She ignored me so I shifted my questions.

"Your folks must have called the police. Didn't they look in the closet?"

"They did, but not carefully. The community was upset about anti-Semitism. Neighbors were feeling unsafe, yelling and reminding the police about the swastikas. At that time, if a Jewish child went missing the police labeled the disappearance as a hate crime. My grandparents were frightened of any authority, especially those in uniform. It was important for Grandpa to hurry the cops out of our apartment."

"But you had information about a child who went missing and you said nothing."

Leah nodded. "Everyone talked about the missing child. It was in all the newspapers and a photo was on local TV. Reporters kept trying to question my parents as well as all the people who lived up and down the block. Nobody was interested in what a kid had to say, and I was glad not to have to reveal anything."

I trailed Leah back to my office where she picked up the album she had left on the couch. Of course, I wondered how her husband and kids would react to her having kept this childhood, life-changing episode from them.

"Look," she said. "Here's a photo of me and my cousin in our kitchen. You can see fire damage near the window. And here's a shot of my mother and aunt."

The two women, one blonde, one brunette, had curled their hair. They were wearing fashionable hats and tailored suits each with a strand of pearls and a pin on the right side of her jacket. They were smiling in a flirty, happy way. These pictures made the people Leah was talking about real. I saw a resemblance between Leah and her aunt.

"Here's one of all of us with my dad who is smoking. He sure did love his cigarettes. And here's another of the family that lived below us," she said. "Their eldest daughter lives in Brooklyn. I don't know where the boys are. I don't even know why we posed together since we weren't close."

"Very nice," I said, watching her place her index finger over the large group photo, circling back to the children.

"I called the police yesterday," she said, closing the album. "Not to tell them my story. I wanted to know what they discovered. They won't give out any information."

"The police won't tell me anything either. That's why I hired a detective. I'm sure John would like to talk to you."

Leah wilted into one of the soft chairs. Her shoulders slumped and she started to weep. "You're the first person I've opened up to, perhaps because you're a stranger. Now you want me to tell a detective!"

25. Remembering

Momism: Try to understand why.

The minute Leah said the dead person in the wall was her fault, repressed memories flashed in front of me like an old silent film. My head felt like it might explode. I walked around the store, only dimly aware that Leah was following me. Then I heard sobs. My sobs, escaping from years ago.

"What's going on?" Leah said, putting her arm around my shoulder.

"I should be comforting you," I said, between gulps of air.

"This isn't about me," she said, gently.

All I could do was nod as I tried to compose myself. Nobody knew my history. Not Kevin. Not my kids. I was amazed that I had buried the truth for practically my whole life, pretending it never happened. But it did.

"I was taking care of my younger sister," I said, my words barely audible. "She was five. I was ten. My father used to joke that Judith was trouble and I was double trouble. Perhaps it was because we were curious, spirited kids constantly getting into mischief. And I was always blamed for any problems. Maybe I deserved it."

Leah handed me a tissue. I dabbed at my eyes as she led me to the back of the store where we sat on my orange couch. It seemed too happy a color for my story.

"One time Dad was at work and Mom had an appointment. The sitter cancelled and since my mother would be back within the hour, she decided to leave us alone. Being the eldest, I was put in charge."

"You were so young to be on your own," she said. "Your mother was responsible for that decision and for anything that happened."

Why are you revealing our secret, I could hear my mother say.

"We lived in a duplex apartment," I said, ignoring Leah's heavy words, not ready to accept her judgment. "There was a staircase leading from the living room to the upstairs bedrooms. My sister and I were in my parents' room trying on old clothes Mom had piled up to give away. It was the '60s and my mother had changed her wardrobe to reflect the times. She no longer wore twinset cardigan sweaters, tea-length swing dresses, cinch belts and tight turquoise capri pants, preferring bell-bottomed jeans and mini-skirts. On her bed I found a dress with puffed shoulders. I put it on, not caring that the full skirt fell beyond my ankles."

"So far, it sounds like a good activity."

"My sister chose a pair of black trousers. I remember watching her put both feet inside one pant leg. Though she held the pants up to her armpits with both hands, the legs fell beyond the ends of her feet. Everything was so big. It made us laugh."

"Something happened to your sister, didn't it?" Leah said softly.

"Not just something," I managed to choke out, barely able to speak. "When Judith stood, she tripped, but managed to stand again. Then the doorbell rang."

I took a deep breath before continuing.

"We were giggling as we turned to race down the stairs. Her feet were still in one of the pant legs so she hopped," I said, recalling our happiness before the awful tragedy played out in my mind.

Leah listened silently.

"Judith turned toward the stairs, trying to be the first to answer the door. Despite hopping, she beat me. Maybe I was being kind and let her go ahead. Suddenly, she stopped. I was so close behind I might have bumped into her. I'm pretty sure I didn't, but maybe I did or maybe that's wishful thinking."

Tears streamed down my face as I paused.

"We both lost our balance. I grabbed the railing. Judith fell. I screamed, watching her tumble down looking like a rag doll, pant legs whirling, arms flailing. She hit the marble floor with a thump. I called to her over and over. She never answered. Never got up. Never said another word. Never laughed."

Leah's grip on my shoulders tightened as she rocked with me.

"It didn't matter that we hadn't answered the front door. Nobody was there. It was just a package that had been delivered. When my mother came home, she found me sitting on the bottom step, staring down at my sister. I have no idea how long I stayed like that. An ambulance was summoned, but it was too late."

We sat silently, while I tried to calm myself. After a few minutes, Leah spoke first.

"How did your family help you get over this catastrophe?"

"Help? We buried my sister immediately and never spoke her name. Never talked about what happened."

Leah hugged me tighter. I knew she understood.

"At school I could hear kids whisper when I came into a room. Sometimes they pointed. In the beginning, my mother cried every time she looked at me. When the school semester ended, we sold the house and moved to a new neighborhood."

I started to sob again, having trouble catching my breath.

"From then on, anyone I met had no idea I once had a sister, a sweet little girl who adored me, who followed me all the time and tried to do everything I did. It was as if Judith never existed. I wasn't allowed to talk about her, couldn't tell anyone how I felt. We never went to visit her grave, nor have I been there as an adult. My mother told me we don't discuss this. Ever."

"It wasn't your fault," Leah said.

"My mother would be so angry right now. I can just see her, hear her telling me, with tight lips, not to tell. Even now, I feel so guilty betraying my mother's trust."

"Your mother was wrong," Leah said. "She's gone now. She can't help and she can't hurt anymore. Whatever comes next is up to you."

"I know, yet I've not been able to break with her. Can you imagine that my husband has no idea I was not an only child? My kids wonder why I'm super protective. They have no clue why I became a helicopter mom, hovering over their every activity."

"I can see how you would be," Leah said.

Her words, said softly, with a knowing compassion, buoyed me. I straightened, still clutching the tissue, drained, yet relieved.

"Tell me, Leah. What happened? Why did you come here?"

Leah pursed her lips, looking at me without speaking, gazing for a moment over my shoulder as if in thought. Just then, my cell phone rang. It was John.

"I have the forensic report," he said. "Can we meet at our favorite coffee shop?"

"Absolutely, and I'll call Kevin. Oh," I said, looking at Leah and speaking as if it were an afterthought, "and I hope to bring Leah, too."

26. Susan and Leah and John and Kevin

Momism: You cannot change what was.

"Hurry up, John," I said, tapping my foot as he folded his tall body into our booth without spilling his large cup of Panera's coffee. "You're taking too long."

When God gave out patience, he sure did skip you, my mother said.

"It's all here," he said, slapping the forensic report on the table.

I think he was enjoying being the messenger.

"And don't ask me how I got it," he said, taking time to make eye contact, nodding toward each one of us, silently securing a promise not to interfere with his methods.

"The skeleton was a child, six to eight years old. Female. Died about sixty-plus years ago. No evidence of violence."

"How do they know?" Kevin said.

"No bashed-in skull or severed limbs. Of course, there might have been harm to her body, her organs, but they deteriorated so like I said, we have no evidence. Her neck was broken, most likely from the fall, probably dropped down the shaft and died immediately upon impact."

I shook my head as if that could change what had happened. Leah touched her neck and began to cry, a quiet weeping. We sat without moving while I waited for her to explain what she knew. I could hear Kevin sip his coffee and John's shoes scrape the floor as he stretched out his legs. Other patrons' voices merged into a distant drone.

"Everyone helped with the search," Leah said, between sniffles.

"What search?" I said.

Kevin nudged me under the table, his way of telling me to just listen. I was glad he didn't say it out loud.

"The family filed a missing person's report. Her photo was printed in the local newspapers and posters were pinned onto telephone poles and buildings. I still have copies folded away in the bottom of a draw. Some people thought she had wandered off and was lost forever."

"Who? Who wandered off?" I said, immediately thinking about the snapshot Leah had shown me yesterday, the one that included their neighbor's children. I remembered her touching it, moving her index finger ever so slowly over the faces of the youngest, then circling the littlest girl again.

"Esther. Esther was missing," Leah said, covering her eyes with her hands then letting out a deep sob. "She was six, one year younger than I was. You saw her face in the photo I showed you yesterday."

"Oh my God," I said, feeling nauseous and craving a chance to hug my daughter.

"I knew searching the area would find nothing," Leah said.

"Why?" Kevin said. "Why do you say that?"

"Esther was old enough to ask for help. She could tell people where she came from if she had gotten lost. Besides, she was too timid to go out alone. She would look out her window and if I were outside, she would join me. We would play together until her older sister, Malka, came to take her home."

Leah folded and unfolded her hands, placed them in her lap then repeated folding and unfolding her hands.

"If I put my crayons in a wooden cheese box, she would dash downstairs to the grocery store to ask for a box. I liked her and I liked her mimicking me. It made me feel important. At the time, I also felt in my gut that what happened was my fault."

"You were a little girl. How could it be your fault?" I said.

"One time, I showed Esther my secret hiding place in our apartment. She giggled and I could tell she enjoyed being let in on my secret, on something special."

"You didn't push her, did you?" I said, afraid to hear her answer.

"Oh God, no!"

"Then why do you think you're to blame?" John said.

"Like I told Susan, the closet was an old laundry chute with a hole in back. Obviously, there was also one in the apartment right below us."

"You think she opened the same closet downstairs, peeked in and fell down," John said, "assuming there was a hole in the back like you had."

"Exactly."

"Didn't you tell your parents what you thought?" John said. His voice was calm, tender, encouraging. I could sense how he must have handled witnesses with the same kind, yet firm, style.

"I told my grandpa," Leah said. "He didn't believe that's what happened. He told me to keep quiet, to let the police do their job. He made me promise never to mention the closet again."

Leah and I looked at each other. I knew we understood one another more than anyone at the table realized.

"He and Grandma had shared so many stories of pogroms in the old country that I became scared of police in uniform," she said. "I was happy not to say anything. Looking back, I think he was trying to protect me from being involved."

I nodded at Leah, wondering if parents who protect their children from horrible events forfeit an opportunity to teach them values and strength.

"Didn't the police question you anyway?"

"I was a kid. Nobody cared what I had to say."

Kevin and John remained still, seeming non-judgmental.

"Didn't someone look in the shaft?" I said, feeling frustrated at what appeared to be police ineptitude.

"One of the first things the police did when they came into our apartment was open the closet door. I watched them look down the hole with a flashlight. They claimed they saw nothing. If they did the same in the downstairs apartment, they didn't look hard enough. They were already convinced it was something that happened outside our home. Maybe they thought the opening wasn't big enough for a person to fall through, though Esther was skinny, like me. Anyway, it was all my fault."

"I still don't understand why you insist on taking responsibility," Kevin said.

"I used to tell jokes. I'd make up something silly then add, 'only kidding.' I told Esther there were magic spirits in the closet, spirits who brought happiness. Esther wanted to see them so I told her I was only teasing. She didn't believe me. She must have tried to find the spirits in the closet in her own home."

"You are not to blame for her curiosity!" John said.

A wave of sorrow enveloped me. Since my first meeting with Leah, identifying the skeleton was no longer a who-done-it game to distract me from my problems that now seemed trivial. The skeleton had become the lovely little girl I had seen in Leah's album, a child cut off from experiencing so many milestones with a mother and father who never knew what transpired.

"I can hardly imagine what the loss did to everyone," I said.

"My mother said Esther's family always hoped the next phone call would bring an answer or the next ring of the doorbell would bring her home," Leah said. "I knew it would never happen."

My mid-life struggle to redefine myself seemed silly in comparison to what I just learned. I put my arms around Leah, offering solace like she had done for me. She curled away.

"All the adults believed she was kidnapped. They were scared Rachel or I would be next if the crazy person who took Esther wasn't found. They enlisted our entire cousins' club to walk the neighborhood asking shop owners if they had seen her. Some offered a reward for information. Members of the shul started a collection to hire a private detective. Most congregants contributed. After three months, except for the immediate family, everyone gave up. Still, Grandpa made me keep quiet."

"He was protective," John said.

"After that, I hated my secret place and vowed never to play hide and seek again."

"What did your family do about the closet?"

"My parents sealed ours," Leah said. "I'm not sure if Esther's did the same. Our apartment no longer felt safe. Photographers and strangers sometimes hovered outside. I heard my mother tell the grocer she was frightened to live in the building. Nobody could understand why I wasn't afraid."

"And to think, it's the same building where *Susanna*'s is. What a sad history," I said.

"My mother was so alarmed she escorted me wherever I went until the summer when we returned to my aunt's hotel in the country," Leah said. "Though this tragedy did not happen to our family, it was so close, there were no more cousins' club meetings or anything joyous for quite a while."

"Did you tell your cousin you thought you were responsible?" I said.

"I wished Rachel had been with me. At the time, she was in a sanitarium getting cured from tuberculosis. She stayed there for two years. When she came back, we all moved to Westchester. Rachel's illness was such a fright, her mother decided to have more children. She became pregnant, and with God's help, had twins. My cousin and I went to a new school. Like you said, a fresh start."

By now, I was weeping quietly. Kevin gave me his handkerchief. It made me think of Roberto.

"On the surface, things looked normal," Leah said. "In some ways, they were. We lived a very ordinary life. Dad worked. Mom took care of the house and me and sewed my clothes. I studied to get into college and then medical school, a way to climb above my family's immigrant beginnings."

By now tears were trickling down Leah's face, yet she held her composure. I felt uncomfortable because our meeting felt less like a coffee shop conversation and more like we were interrogating her.

"Nothing was as it used to be," she said. "I thought that as I grew up, I wouldn't have so many fears, no more worries about polio or tuberculosis or an atom bomb, or authority figures in uniform, but there was always something hanging over my head that I didn't talk about. I never told Rachel that Esther's death was my fault, and we used to tell each other everything. I have carried my secret for more than sixty years."

She took a deep breath. I did the same.

"What others think is my strength, quietly achieving my goals, is really my weakness, my way of concealing anything painful."

None of us said anything. What could we say?

"Every year I light a memorial candle for Esther. What happened has gnawed at me ever since she disappeared. When newspapers recently mentioned the skeleton, it all flooded back. Maybe it's not legally my fault, not a crime that I committed, but on some level, I do believe I'm to blame for what happened."

"It was an accident," I said. "If one of us, God forbid, gets hit by a car crossing the street after this meeting, would you think it was my fault for bringing us here today?"

"It's not the same. Esther knew about the hiding place because of me. She believed happy spirits were inside. I've had to live with that my whole life."

"You might as well also blame the landlord for not sealing the closet," Kevin said. "Or the last tenant for not fixing the floors. If you think like that, they're just as guilty."

"That's a bit far-fetched for me," Leah said, "though I'll consider your point, try to hold onto it if I can. I guess it's time to tell the police."

"Leah," John said, smoothing back the top of his hair, "the police don't need to hear your secret. Sixty years ago, there was a bizarre accident, a no-fault situation. Case closed."

Maybe it was closed officially, but Leah's quiet suffering affected me more than I wanted to admit. Esther would never marry like my Sean, whose choice suddenly seemed good enough for me to give it a chance. Esther would never have children like my Jennifer planned to have later in her life. Now, freezing eggs felt like taking advantage of modern technology, not a reason to fight.

John shut the folder with the forensic information and handed it to Leah.

"If you go to the police you can claim some items I believe are yours—two gold chains, each with a Star of David and an old shoe bag containing 19 silver dollars. The cops were trying to figure out the significance of 19."

"They're from my dad. One for every A I earned in school. Rachel told me she was playing with them in the chute and then dropped the bag."

"She'll be glad to learn you got them back," I said.

"She would be, except she passed away eight years ago. Emphysema. Weak lungs. Smoked too much. Something our parents encouraged despite her history of TB. By the time everyone knew how harmful tobacco is, Rachel was addicted."

"And the gold chains?"

"One must be Rachel's, the other, Esther's," Leah said. "I should bring the necklace to Malka, Esther's sister, but don't think I can face her. I keep waiting for something terrible to happen to me, a punishment for what I did. Malka and I didn't like each other. Maybe seeing her again will be my punishment."

"It sounds like you're thinking that life is a sequence with one event building upon another," Kevin said. "And eventually our past catches up with us."

Leah shrugged. Her shoulders seemed to relax for the first time.

Mine contracted. Maybe life is a chain of events and my past was about to catch up with me, too. If I hadn't gotten fired, I wouldn't have traveled to Italy alone. If I had not gone alone, I would not have befriended Roberto—or his wife, who became my dress designer. I would not have opened a boutique and found a new career and discovered the skeleton that brought me here with Leah. Maybe all events in life are linked.

Perhaps I can move on, stop wallowing and learn how to enjoy the next phase of my journey. At the same time, my thoughts seemed like psychobabble, pulling me back to my time with Roberto in Florence. It would be hard to tell Kevin everything, but also a relief not to use energy to keep things hidden. It would also be a relief for Leah to tell Esther's sister what she knew, no matter how difficult.

"I'll go with you," I said, surprising myself.

"Where?"

"To visit Malka. Maybe if you're not alone it will be easier. No guarantee. At least you can lean on me if necessary. I won't say anything, just be your support. And you'll be free of your secret."

I wanted to do the same, free myself by washing away Roberto and telling my family about my sister. I repeated the words "my sister," bringing her back into my life.

27. Susan and Leah Visit Esther's Sister

Momism: You get what you need.

"Does Malka know we're coming?" I said, as Leah and I drove along the Belt Parkway toward Brooklyn. "I tracked down her phone number and contacted her last night. Of course, my call took her by surprise."
"I assume you mentioned the skeleton."
"No, I didn't."
"Why does she think we're visiting?" I said, feeling a little uncomfortable.
"I told her I had news about Esther. She kept asking me to tell her right away, on the phone. I refused, so she yelled at me, just like she did when we were kids. The minute Malka bullied me, I used to give in. This time, I insisted we speak in person."
"You told her you were bringing a friend, right?"
"No. The less I say, the better. She'll see you when we get there."
Now I had mixed feelings about tagging along, but it was too late to change plans.
The minute Malka opened her door, I was surprised she grabbed Leah in a hug. After what Leah had told me, Malka's greeting was warmer than I expected, with no indication they shared a hostile history. I stepped back watching them grasp the past before stopping to take a good look at each other.

They were about the same height, though Malka looked substantially older with gray and white hair. While Leah was fashionably elegant in a subdued way, Malka's rimless glasses, timeless black skirt and white blouse that covered her well-fed, soft body, fit my preconceived image of an elderly, old-fashioned grandmother.

"Hello trouble," Malka said, easing her words with a laugh. "What's it been, sixty years? Maybe more. I would recognize you anywhere. Still so skinny. Come in."

The fragrance of something freshly baked surrounded us as we entered the apartment, a hospitable contrast to the grave purpose of our visit. Malka and I shook hands while Leah introduced me as her friend, nothing more.

"It was shocking when you called. Really," Malka said, leading us into the living room. "All this time and neither one of us ever reached out. Sixty years and no word, no contact. It's good to see you. It's also bittersweet. Just your presence brings up thoughts of my little sister."

Leah nodded as they sat on opposite ends of a brocade, cream-colored couch that had ornately carved wooden legs and arms. These two women shared childhood memories, both joyous and tragic. I tried to fade into the matching chair, there, but not there.

"You still scared of me, Leah? Is that why you brought her?" Malka said, moving her wrist and pointing her thumb at me.

Leah grunted a half laugh, twisting her fingers together in her lap. I was glad not to be the one to tell this woman about her sister, glad to be around just for support.

"Tell me, how are your brothers?" Leah said, shifting the conversation. "Where are they now?"

I could sense she was stalling.

"All good," Malka said, cutting out all family history, placing a strand of gray hair behind her ear that had escaped from her bun.

"And you, Malka?" Leah said.

"Married young, right out of high school to that redheaded boy I was friends with from around the corner. I lost him three years ago. Cancer." Malka pointed to a row of photos on an end table. "We had three boys and I have six grandchildren I see every Friday night for Shabbat dinner. That's the short version. Now, tell me about you and your family."

Leah took a deep breath.

"Where should I begin? You know we moved to Westchester when Rachel came home from the sanitarium. I'm a doctor, a pulmonary specialist. Should have retired by now. I still keep a few patients and give lectures. I'm married and having been an only child, I wanted more than one. We have three children and also have six grandchildren. We try to get together every Sunday, though it's rare when everyone can make it."

Their chatter sounded reserved, a necessary filler before tackling what happened to Esther. We sat quietly, awkward for a few moments, until Malka broke the silence.

"Would you like some coffee or tea? And cake?" she said, getting up slowly, as if her bones ached. "I did much of the cooking as a teen. Mama was the baker. She kept her recipes in a binder and after she passed, I tried them all."

"I'd love to taste your cake," I said, realizing this was not the right time to count calories.

"I remember your mother's desserts," Leah said. "Esther used to bring some to me whenever she came upstairs to play."

"When I asked everyone where the cake went, my sister always told me she ate more," Malka said, pursing her lips and shaking her head. "So, enough chitchat. I'm ready to hear why you came here."

There it was. Our painful message ready to be revealed.

Leah folded and unfolded her hands. She smoothed out her knee-length Max Mara skirt, looked up then back down at her knees. I sat quietly, viewing the heavy furniture, avoiding my reflection in the mirror facing the couch, waiting for Leah to reveal the details that I knew had to be told in whatever way she felt best. Her next comment threw me.

"Tell her about your store," Leah said.

"Me?" It was my turn to take a deep breath. There were enough delays without my going off on a tangent about my boutique.

"Yes, you. Tell her about the renovations."

Since Malka knew nothing, I guessed Leah wanted me to explain my involvement, the reconstruction leading up to the horrific discovery.

"I rented two stores in the building you used to live in," I said. "I'm opening a boutique selling upscale women's fashions from Italy."

I waited for a reaction, picking up crumbs from my plate, then putting them down. Since nobody said anything, I continued.

"Leah told me there used to be a grocery on the ground floor. It was gone long before I rented."

Nerves made me speak too rapidly. Malka nodded while sitting straight with no expression, much like a teacher listening to a kid's excuse for not doing homework.

"Tell her about the wall," Leah said.

I looked at her, then at Malka. So much for just being supportive.

"I wanted more space, so I broke down the connecting wall," I said.

Malka remained quiet.

"Tell her what you found," Leah said, pushing me to keep going.

If Leah blindsided me like this at the ad agency, I might have fired her. But this was not a corporation, this was life. Despite my apprehension, I felt compassion for her. Still, there was no easy way to say what came next. I whispered it quickly. "At the bottom of the wall was a skeleton."

"What?" Malka said, sitting up even straighter, then leaning toward me. "Esther. It's Esther, isn't it?"

"We think so," I said, reaching toward the couch to hold her hand. "Didn't you read about the skeleton in the papers?"

"No. I avoid the news. Too depressing."

"A detective I hired is sure the police will want to do a DNA test," I said. "To confirm the connection."

"You hired a detective?" Malka said.

"Well, it's my store. I needed to find answers, at first for myself. Now, for you and your brothers—and for Leah."

Malka pulled her hand away and put her fist to her heart, saying something in Hebrew. I didn't know what she was saying. Perhaps she was praying. I sure felt her emotions. To claim this was a life-changing moment would be melodramatic. At the same time, it was very difficult. It seemed like forever before Malka was able to collect her thoughts and speak.

"How did she get into the wall?" she said, in an angry tone, as if it were my fault this happened to her sister.

"We think she fell down the laundry chute," I said, looking at Leah, hoping she would take over the conversation.

"What laundry chute? I did the laundry. There was no chute," Malka said.

"It was hidden behind an unused closet door in our apartment. I assume it must have been the same in your place," Leah said.

"There was a closet door. It was always closed," Malka said shaking her head. "Nobody used it and I never tried to open it."

I wanted to hold Malka, but felt she would not like to be so close. At the same time, Leah was shaking. Maybe she was the one I should embrace.

"Was the wall where the laundry chute used to be?" Malka said.

"It appears that way," Leah said.

"How did Esther know it existed? How did she get inside?"

"We're getting to that," Leah said, then turned to me again. Before I could say anything, Malka continued. "Esther disappeared when I was 15. The police questioned the whole family, including me. I told them about three boys I saw painting anti-Jewish slogans and Nazi swastikas on the synagogue. Everyone was sure someone in this group had kidnapped my sister."

"So, the police thought this was a hate crime," I said.

"Yes, though I don't remember them using those exact words. My parents worried I would be grabbed next. Your parents feared the same for you," she said, facing Leah. "That's why we were never allowed out by ourselves. It was hard because at 15, I wanted time alone with my friends."

"Were those boys found and punished?" I said.

"No. Nobody was ever identified concerning the swastikas or Esther's disappearance. Mama was heartbroken and clung to me as well as my brothers. She cried for Esther and cried because we couldn't have a proper burial without a body."

"Well, at least you now know she wasn't kidnapped," I said, feeling this information would not provide any comfort. "If the DNA matches, the police probably will give you her remains." I couldn't believe these harsh words were coming out of my mouth when all I wanted to do was sob and hold Malka.

"It will prove that Esther fell down the laundry chute," Leah said with tears streaming down her cheeks.

I was confident here's where Leah would step up and share her story. Instead, she moved her head in my direction again.

"Tell her," Leah said to me. "Tell her about my hiding place and my jokes and magic spirits."

Leah was a doctor. She must be used to difficult conversations with patients, sometimes informing families when a loved one doesn't survive. I believed she should be capable of divulging this story.

"You tell her, Leah. It's your experience and your memory. Malka needs to hear it from you."

"I can't," Leah said, lowering her head as more tears fell onto her pale gray silk blouse creating a pattern of salty circles. "I haven't told anyone in all these years. I can't do it."

"Leah, you haven't changed," Malka said, shaking her head. "Still a big shot with your ideas, like coming here to tell me something, then passing it on to someone else. You always got Esther into trouble. I need to shake you or grab you by the arm, to straighten you out and get you to do the right thing, just like I used to."

Leah sobbed like a little girl. I wanted to get out of there, but it was up to me to pitch in for my new friend.

"You must be a good person," Malka said to me. "Coming here with Leah to bring me such news."

The words, "good person" rang loudly in my ears and settled in my heart.

"Okay, I'll tell you what Leah told me." I turned toward Leah. "If you promise to interrupt if I leave anything out. All the facts need to be conveyed and you are the only one who knows it all."

I then relayed the whole story, omitting the magic spirits and Leah's habit of telling jokes. I didn't believe the accident was Leah's fault and therefore refused to create a grisly atmosphere of blame. Those details wouldn't serve any good purpose.

Suddenly, Malka broke into my thoughts, screaming, "It's my fault. It's all my fault."

"How is it your fault?" I said, totally confused.

"I was the eldest and therefore in charge of watching my brothers and sister when Mama did her errands. I should have been more aware. Should have seen Esther start to climb into the closet we never opened. I should have stopped her."

"Malka, she could just as easily have gone in there when your mother was home," Leah said. "Esther was full of mischief and loved to do whatever she felt like doing, especially behind your back or when your mother wasn't looking."

Malka shook her head.

"Esther never listened to rules. That's one of the reasons we had so much fun together," Leah said. "You have no idea if she fell during your watch."

"There's another reason it's my fault," Malka said. "I saw the three boys who painted the swastikas. The cops believed me and didn't consider anything else. Without my story, maybe they would have looked more carefully in all parts of our home and found her in time to get her out."

"Nobody could have saved her," I said. "The forensic report says she most likely broke her neck during the fall and died immediately."

The minute I said this, I felt sorry. Though it's my style to be blunt, to say things as they are, the vision was gruesome. I didn't want to be the one who brought this forward.

"She was right there all the time," Malka moaned. "My mother always hoped Esther was alive somewhere. Leah, why didn't you tell my family about the laundry chute? How could you keep this to yourself?"

"I told my grandfather the day your sister went missing. He was adamant that I keep quiet. He felt my idea was impossible and that I should stay away from the authorities. I was a little girl and listened to him. I was glad not to have to speak up because maybe I would be blamed for this terrible accident. I thought I would be sent to jail."

"Nobody would send a kid to jail. It's been sixty years. You've had plenty of time to find me and say something. What's the matter with you?" Malka said, pointing her index finger at Leah, who seemed to shrivel up.

"At least she's here now," I said.

"Susan left out an important detail. It's the reason I feel I might be responsible," Leah said.

Leah took a deep breath, got up and started to pace around the room.

"I told Esther there were magic spirits in my hiding place upstairs. Although I let her know I was only joking, she must have tried to find them. I think she fell in while looking down the chute in your apartment. If yours was like ours, there was a partial floor and a hole in the back."

"You both have to stop blaming yourselves for a freak accident," I said. Neither woman was listening to me.

"Did you come here so I would forgive you?" Malka said. "If so, I cannot. It's not up to me to absolve anyone. I can't even forgive myself."

"I realize nobody can excuse me," Leah said. "Believe me, I have searched for solace all these years. I only came here to share what happened."

"At least you've given my family closure. I thank you for that. Of course, I shall go to the police for a DNA test and assuming it matches, we can have a proper burial. Oy, poor Esther."

"I brought you this," Leah said, taking the necklace out of her handbag before getting ready to flee the discomfort that filled the room. "It was found around your sister's neck."

Malka folded the necklace in her hand and brought it to her heart. Now both women were crying. Though I felt their pain, I never knew the little girl who lost her life. I didn't want to be disrespectful by pushing myself into their space, so I waited with my head bent while they embraced and I said a silent prayer for my sister, Judith.

On the way back to Manhattan, Leah appeared pensive.

"Maybe I shouldn't have told Malka about my joke or about the magic spirits," she said. "It made me feel better, but did nothing positive for her. She still blamed herself for not noticing her sister going into the closet. Maybe some secrets should not be shared."

28. Susan and Kevin

Momism: Growing old makes you wise, sometimes.

"You should have told me when we first met," Kevin said, as we were getting ready to go to the cemetery.
    "I know, but you couldn't make it better. You couldn't fix the pain. And my mother had a choking hold on me concerning Judith."
    "I might have understood why you're so protective of Jennifer and Sean, been more of a friend and less of a critic. I might even have been able to offer some solace to your mom while she was alive."
    "Impossible," I said, "regardless of how much she adored you."
    "Is Jennifer named after her?"
    "In my mind, she is."
    "Have you ever visited your sister's grave?"
    "The only two times I was near her gravesite was when we buried my parents, first my father, then my mother five years later."
    "I was with you. I didn't see a tombstone with her name."
    "Judith's grave is off to the side. I waved. I should have acknowledged her years ago, but that would have included breaking my mother's spell. I didn't have the guts while Mom was alive. After she died, it became even harder. Now that you know about Judith,

everything feels different. Freer. And it's all thanks to Leah."

"It's so nice that she wants to join us today," Kevin said, holding up two of his sweaters for me to choose for him to wear.

"The blue," I said, then smiled, thinking about my new friend.

"Leah's very strong. She choreographed the meeting with Malka so that I was the one who had to tell Esther's sister almost everything."

"That must have been a challenge with your get-to-the-point, brisk style. How'd you manage such a delicate conversation?"

"Bluntly, I hate to admit. I was so shocked to be put on the spot, I didn't have time to think about my delivery."

"What's Malka like?"

"Quite a mixture. She's older than Leah, but she seemed even more elderly than I expected, moving slowly, speaking carefully. On first sight, she looks like an old-fashioned, soft grandmother: gray hair in a bun, oversized body covered by sedate, loose clothing. She gives the impression of someone who can easily take care of everything and everyone. I immediately warmed up to her. Then, during our time together, her personality shifted."

"How so?"

"Initially, she was nice. Malka and Leah hugged, which seemed normal. Afterwards, they reminisced in a superficial way, catching up on sixty years in one or two sentences each, dancing around the reason for our visit. Malka had even baked a cake."

"Did you eat it?" Kevin said, with a mischievous grin.

"Of course. It wasn't the time to diet. I felt as if I were watching a movie unfold, a piece of fiction brought to life by a cast of characters including me. Except it was real."

I paused to find a comfortable pair of flats in one of my walk-in closets.

"Later, Malka became abrupt," I said, returning from my shoe collection without missing a beat. "As expected, she was shocked to learn what happened, amazed that Leah kept her secret all these years."

"I can relate to that," Kevin said. "Under the circumstances, she needs to be forgiven."

I nodded, understanding that Kevin might also be referring to his initial explosive reaction upon learning about Judith. In all our years together, I had never seen him so angry or hurt. For quite some time he remained silent. Then he kept asking questions, wondering if I had other secrets, criticizing me for misrepresenting myself as an honest woman, making me the one who needed to be forgiven. I got it. I apologized, but my words felt weak. Eventually, he was able to become supportive.

"How did Leah manage to involve you?" he said.

"Leah asked me to tell Malka about my store. At first, I couldn't understand why. Then I realized she wanted me to share information about the renovations because that would introduce the bones. By the way, I no longer think of our discovery as a skeleton. From the time I first saw her photo, the bones became Esther. They'll always be Esther."

"So, you're even more involved than before. Emotionally, that is," he said, grabbing a navy single-breasted blazer.

I nodded, eyes lowered, fist to heart like Malka had done.

"I guess revealing everything to me was easier for Leah than telling Malka or her husband and kids," I said. "It makes me wonder if most couples, even happy ones, keep parts of their past tucked away."

"Leah's probably relieved to have shed her burden. It wouldn't surprise me if part of the reason she's coming today is to make sure you've done the same. For sure, keeping a secret can affect one's health and one's soul," Kevin said, flicking some of Max's hairs off his jacket.

Soul. That was pretty philosophical for my husband who is usually the voice of reason. I wanted to lie down on our bed next to him, cuddle into his arms with Max at our feet, a picture of perfection, but Jennifer, Sean, Sophie and Leah would arrive at any moment.

"The difficulties of this visit are consuming me," I said. "It feels as if Leah will be helping me as much as I might have helped her."

That's absurd, my mother said, still popping up in my head. *Leah's life is not your life. Don't read anything into simple acts of kindness.*

"I'm happy you went with her. It's exactly what a good person would do," Kevin said, giving me a hug. "It's something you'd have done before your brain got rattled when you lost your job."

"I told Malka the rest of the story, starting with our discovery of Esther and working backwards to what

Leah had shared with me. I left out the jokes and spirits. When I finished, Malka started claiming the accident was her fault."

"Her fault? How was that possible?"

"She was babysitting and it happened on her watch. Malka and Leah each claim responsibility. As an outsider, it appears to me that Esther had a mind of her own and neither one is to blame."

"Well, from what you told me, it appears that your sister, Judith, also had a mind of her own," Kevin said, continuing to embrace me in a hug. "Sounds like she raced to the top of the stairs all by herself, intent on getting there ahead of you, then accidentally tripped on the oversized outfit she was wearing."

"I know you're trying to help, but I'm not sure I can accept your interpretation. I was taking care of my sister and just like Malka, it happened while I was babysitting. That's what my mom told me."

"Mothers are not always right."

I didn't respond. There was nothing to say, so I grabbed my handbag and summoned the elevator.

At the cemetery, I let Kevin hold my arm, offering encouragement I thought I didn't need. It felt good to approach Judith together. Jennifer, Sean, Sophie and Leah walked more slowly behind us.

We stopped at my parents' graves first. Leah looked around and found a small, smooth oval rock that she placed on my mother's tombstone. She found another for my father and a third for Judith.

We all followed her lead, including Sophie. Using our left hands, we placed the stones as an act of remembrance, an ancient Jewish tradition signifying that the deceased has not been forgotten. If I had been alone,

I would have indulged my wish to put dozens of rocks on my sister's headstone, one for every year I had missed. As a family, this was all I would do today, promising myself I'd return soon.

29. Today or not Today
Momism: What's done is done.

"Susan, I'm so happy now. We're in such a good place," Kevin said, while chopping lettuce and slicing tomatoes. "It feels like the old days."

It was nice to prepare dinner with my husband in a calm way, to talk about recent developments as the dear friends we are.

"After the belated memorial service, I don't think Malka and Leah will see each other again," I said. "Evidently, they never got along way back when."

"What about you and Leah? Do you think you'll see her again?"

"Not only will I see her, she'll probably be one of my best new friends."

By now, Kevin and I were seated side by side at our kitchen island, drinking club soda and munching on our salad and leftover cold chicken. Max was resting comfortably at Kevin's feet. It was delightfully mundane.

"From what you've told me, I think both women feel comfort knowing what really happened," Kevin said, turning to face me. "Each one can decide it's the other person's fault and pretend not to be accountable."

"I don't think they can pretend anything. At least Esther's heartbreaking death has closure," I said, while tapping my foot against the base of my tall chair.

"They tried to erase the tragedy for years. I guess hiding things never works."

"Like my mother trying to deny my sister's existence," I said, putting down my fork, stopping to express my feelings as clearly as possible. "That didn't work, either. I'm not going to follow that path. I'm going to put everything out in the open. At the same time, I don't intend to relive past problems."

"I'm sure your boutique will provide enough new challenges."

"At least they'll be different. When I first rented my store, I told you I hoped this venture would fill the vacancy that often left me searching for more meaning in the middle of my life. In addition to a new business and new friend, the events surrounding my boutique have helped me create a better attitude. I'm ready to embrace whatever my chain of events leads me to."

"Chain of events? Uh oh. I hear a philosophy coming on. Are you going to tell me to Be Here Now?"

"Not exactly. It's just that I'm determined to move forward and enjoy new experiences," I said, picking at a piece of chicken.

"Well, if what I say counts at all, I think being your own boss will give us more time together. You can manage your schedule," he said, with a wink. "Squeeze in a noontime quicky like we did when you were at the ad agency."

The memory made me smile. We clinked glasses, took a sip and kissed.

"First, I need to figure out how to stop beating up on myself as things change because I'm getting older."

Don't we all, my mom chimed in.

"Oh, for a moment I thought it might be something deep," Kevin said, laughing.

"I'm serious. Please don't mock me. I know I've accomplished a lot, but there's so much more to do while time is flying by. And my dreams keep changing. How can I reach a goal that's amorphous?

"Let's start with that do-good idea and invite John and Nancy to dinner."

"And Sophie," I said. "Don't forget Sophie and Sean."

"And Jennifer and Adam."

"Maybe we can have a family gathering once a week," I said. "It's something Malka and Leah mentioned as one of the ways they've been able to stay engaged with their grandchildren."

"Sounds like a plan."

"By the way, Jennifer is letting me come with her when she retrieves her eggs."

"Progress for the two of you," he said, lifting his glass again.

Just then the phone rang. It was Roberto. I visualized being naked in bed with him without doing anything sexual—that's not cheating. Kevin saw naked women all the time. Part of his work.

It's not the same, Mom said. *And you know it. If I recall, you weren't naked. You kept on your La Perla underwear.*

I hated Mom's spot-on comments when she was alive. She was even more annoying now. Still haunting me with her insights and rules of behavior. Just one kiss wasn't so bad, right?

230

He had garlic breath. Was that why you pulled away? Mom said. *Or was it the sweet smell of the roses your husband had sent?*

The whole episode was gnawing at me. I wanted to divulge my escapade. I wanted to be forgiven.

Don't you dare, I heard my mother say. *Your marriage will never be the same.*

Her warning wasn't necessary. I had already come to that conclusion.

Unburdening herself brought Leah peace. If I unburden myself, I would bring havoc, or at least a loss of trust within my marriage. Leah's situation and Judith were far more serious. The secrets shouldn't be compared.

"*Ciao, Susanna,*" Roberto said, cheery as ever. "Francesca and I are planning another visit to New York, before the Christmas holidays, when Francesca's new designs are scheduled to arrive."

"Lovely," I said, then tried to mouth the gist of the conversation to Kevin.

"Which days are the best?" Roberto said. "How long should we stay?"

"Give me a few days to check my calendar and talk to Kevin. The spring flowers are just blooming," I said, looking out the window at the daffodils along the center of Park Avenue. "There's no rush to decide."

I hung up, grateful there were many months before their next visit. No need for my perfect nose job and me to tell Kevin about my secret. No need to share it now. Not today. Not yet.

Reader Invitation

Susan's mom gave her much advice. I call those gems Momisms and they are listed below. If you have any bits of advice your mom gave you, I invite you to share them. Email your Momisms along with your name to me at: mgottlieb@crescendogroup.com

1. *Expect the unexpected.*
2. *Never force anything*
3. *Understand the other side.*
4. *Relationships are complicated.*
5. *Family is everything.*
6. *Perfect is different for everyone.*
7. *Secrets are meant to be kept.*
8. *Finish what you start.*
9. *Shake your sins of the past.*
10. *The past matters.*
11. *Don't judge a book by its cover.*
12. *Don't share everything.*
13. *Every marriage is different.*
14. *You're never too old to find a new friend.*
15. *Try to understand why.*
16. *You cannot change what was.*
17. *You get what you need.*
18. *Growing old makes you wise, sometime.*
19. *What's done is done.*

Marilyn Gottlieb began her writing career as a columnist for *Dan's Papers* on Long Island, New York. She was SVP, Director of Public Relations and a member of the 17-person Operations Committee for Lintas, a $1.8 billion worldwide advertising agency that was part of The Interpublic Group of Companies. Prior to that she was with Ogilvy & Mather and the American Association of Advertising Agencies. Inducted into the YWCA's prestigious Academy of Women Achievers, she also was an adjunct professor at the New School University and a member of the Board of Advertising Women of New York. Ms. Gottlieb attended Skidmore College and earned an MA from New York University and an MFA in Writing and Literature from Stony Brook Southampton. Her first book was *Life with an Accent* (2013). The young adult version came out in early 2016 and was published in Israel in Hebrew. Her novels include *Dance Me Younger* and the sequel, *Girl in the Wall*. Her next novel, *Beautiful Lunatic*, is forthcoming.

Made in the USA
Middletown, DE
23 April 2022